AF244458

THE NIGHT'S VIOLIN

✢ ✢ ✢

SAGAS of IRTH

Of Swords and Sorrows

The Wrath of Shadows

The Night's Violin

Beyond the Ivory Shore

Upon the Serpent's Tongue

The Twilight Isle

Lady Midnight

The Song of the Sorians

The Iron Knight

NOSETOUCH PRESS
Chicago · Pittsburgh

The Night's Violin

© Copyright 2021 Dane Vale
All Rights Reserved.

ISBN-13: 978-1-944286-15-6

Published by Nosetouch Press
Chicago, Illinois 60611

www.nosetouchpress.com

For more information, contact Nosetouch Press:
info@nosetouchpress.com

Cataloging-in-Publication Data
Names: Vale, Dane, author.
Title: The Night's Violin
Description: Chicago, IL : Nosetouch Press [2021]
Identifiers: ISBN: 9781944286156 (paperback)
Subjects: LCSH: Fantasy — Fiction.
GSAFD: Fantasy fiction. | BISAC: FICTION / Fantasy.

Maps © 2021 by Dane Vale
All Rights Reserved.

Cover, interior, and map design/formatting by Christine M. Scott, Clever Crow Consulting and Design.
www.clevercrow.com

for Dean,
always so high strung.
❖ ❖ ❖

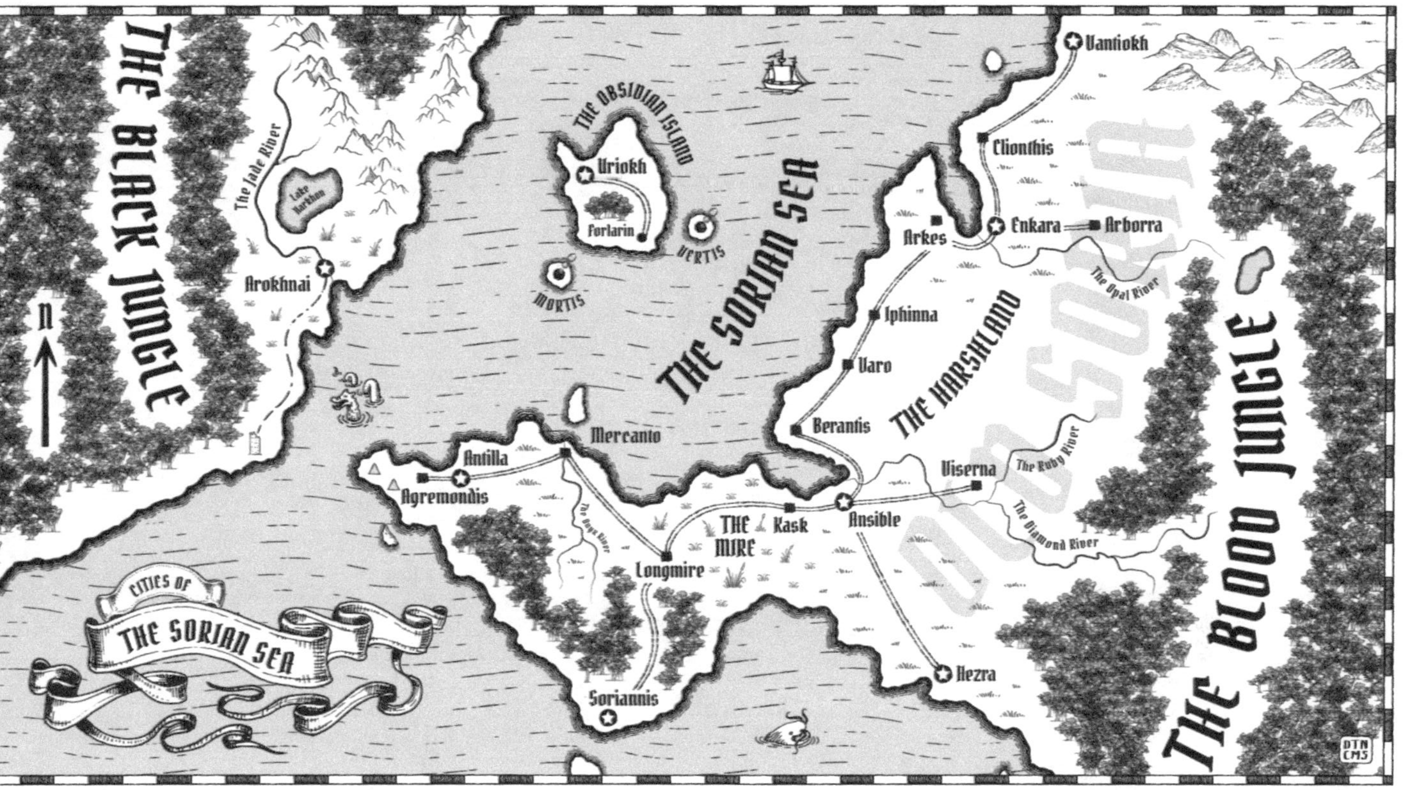

THE BLACK JUNGLE
OLD SORIA
THE BLOOD JUNGLE
THE SORIAN SEA
THE HARSHLAND
THE OBSIDIAN ISLAND
N
Vantiokh
Clionthis
Enkara
Arborra
Arkes
Iphinna
Uaro
Berantis
Viserna
Ansible
Hezra
Uriokh
Forlarin
Vertis
Mortis
Arokhnai
Mercanto
Antilla
Agremondis
Longmire
Soriannis
THE Kask MIRE
The Jade River
Lake Narkhon
The Opal River
The Ruby River
The Diamond River
The Onyx River
CITIES OF
THE SORIAN SEA
DTN
CMS

Table of Contents

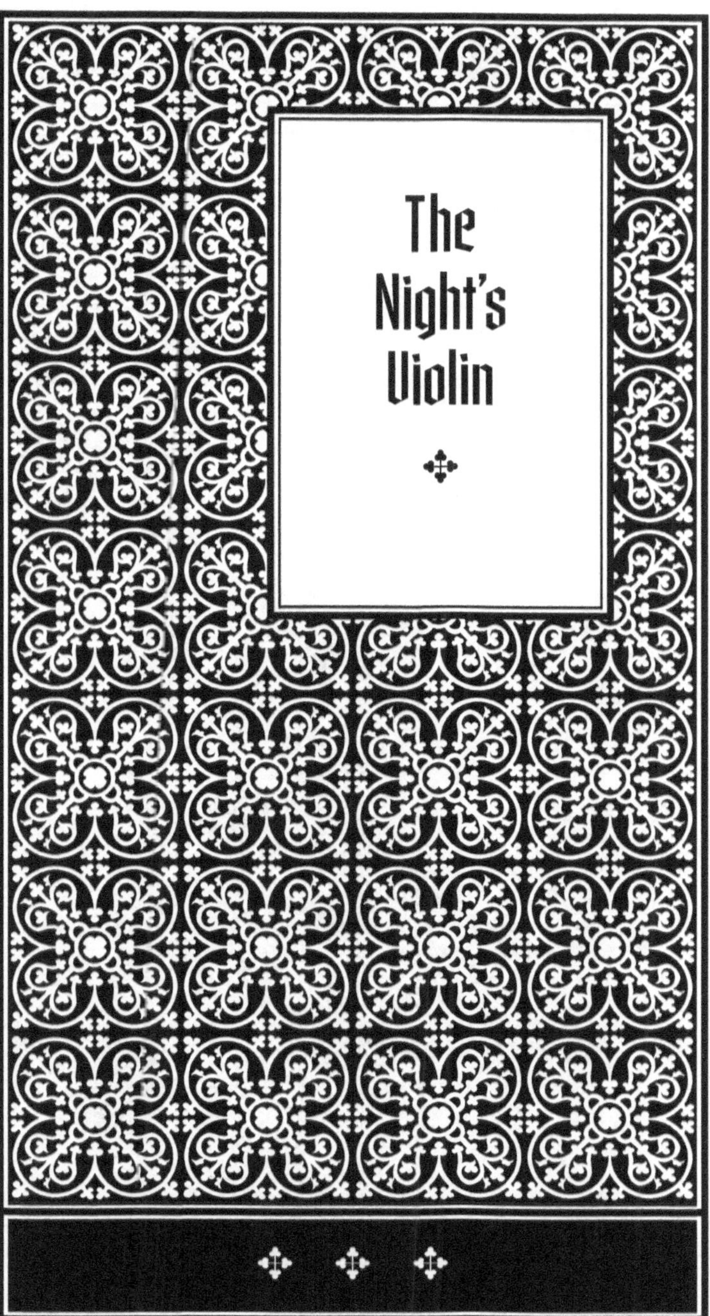

The
Night's
Violin

One

In the fog-drenched Arokhnai pre-dawn, a dozen armed men marched around the Artisan Quarter, carrying spears and swords, their well-oiled black leather armor creaking. They were not part of the City Watch, but were, instead, warriors of the faraway Obsidian Island.

Their commander, Barvikh Abbasa, was not tall, but he was swift and strong. He wore a well-trimmed, chest-nut-colored beard, and had slate blue eyes. The veteran of scores of campaigns on the Obsidian Island, he spoke with the curtness of mercenary professionalism characteristic of a highborn son of the Slaver City of Uriokh, the Obsidiander capital.

"Which way to the luthier?" Barvikh said aloud, hating the taste of the word. The black-cloaked scout, a young woman with short black hair and silver eyes, turned her sharp features toward him, as if he were a nuisance to be brushed away, like the plentiful swampflies that haunted the land approaches to Arokhnai.

Uriokh was a sworn enemy and trade rival of Arokhnai. In fact, Uriokh's proud and daring corsairs plied the waters of the Sorian Sea with a fierce territoriality, seeking to claim prizes and slaves from the merchant republic whenever it could.

Arokhnai had, of late, taken to sailing east, along the coastal cities of Old Soria, rather than risking the northerly route that would take it past Uriokh and her Slavelords.

"The luthier is not far," she said, guiding the men down Arokhnai's narrow alleys that characterized the Artisan Quarter. Space was precious in the mercantile city, especially here. In this place, armies of guildsmen and artisans packed themselves tightly in hope of selling their wares to the rich, privileged, and powerful. Which, by her reckoning, seemed to be most everyone in Arokhnai, which was a uniquely prosperous city.

It was different in Uriokh, where artisan slaves toiled for their freedom for the pleasure of their corsair masters. As one of the oldest and proudest of Slaver Cities, ancient Uriokh viewed the free republic of Arokhnai and its shadowy overlords as an abomination and a menace to their way of life.

"This sort of work is beneath me, Darha," Barvikh said. "I am a warrior prince among my people. You know this."

And he was. His father, Lord Korg Abbasa, had entrusted him to this mission, to accompany the sorceress Darha to Arokhnai to recover the precious artifact that their spies had revealed had come to the city.

"If only you knew," Darha said, putting a slender white finger to her lips, nodding in the direction of the darkened shop. In the front of the whitestone and saffron stucco store hung an old, weatherworn violin from some copper chains well-girded with patina. Above that was a wrought iron balcony in the manner of so many residences in the city.

This time of morning, the City of Arokhnai slept as deeply as it ever did, and the company of warriors held the street for their own, without sign of others. All the same, Barvikh sent three of his men to either end of the street, to ensure that they were not interrupted.

Darha crept close to the luthier's door, holding a hand up to stop Barvikh and his men. They all heeded her as if she'd cast a spell upon them. She listened a moment, before resting a pale palm on the door's lock.

Whispering something in an unfamiliar tongue, she made the lock spring open. Darha stepped aside to let Barvikh and his warriors swarm into the luthier's dwelling, blades drawn and blackened spears hoisted.

Once they were all in, she followed, softly closing the door. The pleasant scent of wood and varnish hung about the dwelling in an artisanal aroma.

Darha drew a smallstone from a purple velvet bag and dropped it into a tiny, rune-bedecked silver lantern, bathing the room in the luminous green glow focused by carefully cut glass panes.

The Obsidiander warriors looked like wights, circulating through the domicile, amid all the shadowy violins that hung from racks, like meat at a butcher's shop. These were men unaccustomed to musicians or instrument makers, beyond what they'd perhaps seen or heard in public markets or carnivals in Uriokh.

Only Darha knew precisely what she was looking for. The warriors circulated through the luthier's dwelling, emerging confused in the lantern light. If there had been blood to be spilled tonight, it wasn't happening in this moment. Barvikh walked up to Darha, who set the little lantern on the luthier's tabletop.

"She's not here," Barvikh said.

"*It's* not here," Darha said. She wove a sigil in the air, and Barvikh felt his stomach clench, reflexively stepping away from the practitioner of magic.

Darha's eyes flashed in the light of the lantern, seeing something other than what was apparent to the warriors, and she daubed her long and slender nose with a burgundy silk kerchief.

"The Black Bard left with it," Darha said. "She went to see someone."

"Who?" Barvikh asked.

Darha said the next word like it was a curse, whispered and sibilant:

"Senator Fiss'Q."

Two

Lyra Longbow, accompanied by the luthier, Kaden Antilla, had petitioned to Fiss'Q for aid before the warriors had appeared at the luthier's door. This amounted to them showing up, seeking an audience at her townhome in the Emerald District.

"We should not have bothered the Senator," Kaden said. "She's a busy and important woman."

"I absolutely have to see her," Lyra said.

"It's unseemly," Kaden said. "Barging in on a Senator this way."

"You can always go back if you're too embarrassed," Lyra said. "I'm not afraid to talk to anyone, no matter who they are."

"No, no," Kaden said. "I'm in her district. Let me make the introduction."

Kaden was white-haired and wiry, bearded with a careworn grimace on his face. He wore a brown artisan's smock, well-stained with varnish and glue.

Lyra could not have looked more distinct from the luthier. She had jet black hair cut short about her shoulders and grey eyes, with a sternly charming bearing that was accentuated by her black doublet, leggings, and well-worn, polished black shoes. She carried an instrument in a black leather case and had a slim, Sylvan-forged rapier at her belt.

An'Alta answered the door, looking at them both a moment. The olive-skinned young woman was the Senator's ward, servant, and apprentice. She gazed at them with big, dark eyes.

"Can I help you?" An'Alta asked.

"Begging your pardon, but we're here to see the Senator," Kaden said.

"I'm Lyra Longbow, the Black Bard," Lyra said. If An'Alta recognized that name, she gave no sign of it. She simply eyed the both warily, before speaking.

"Mistress, we have visitors," she said.

Fiss'Q worked her way downstairs, wearing a silk robe of purple that was festooned with golden runes that danced across the robe in intricate and mesmerizing patterns. As ever, Fiss'Q looked darkly elegant, lean of limb with long black hair and dusky skin, red eyes and the hint of fangs playing about her smile. Her expression was one of the bemusement that invariably danced upon the faces of the otherworldly Shadowlanders, the rulers of the Republic of Arokhnai.

"Then, by all means, let them in," Fiss'Q said, looking at the visitors in turn, her fangs dimpling her lips.

Lyra and Kaden entered, Lyra speaking for them both.

"Senator Fiss'Q," Lyra said. "I'm Lyra, and this is my friend, Kaden."

"Kaden Antilla, the luthier," Fiss'Q said. "I know of you and your fine work."

The luthier looked sheepish.

"Thank you, Senator," Kaden said. "I didn't want Miss Longbow to disturb you with her problem, but she was very insistent that I take her to you."

Lyra gave Kaden a sidelong glance before addressing Fiss'Q.

"I'm sorry to trouble you, Senator, but I just couldn't wait," Lyra said.

"It's no trouble at all," Fiss'Q said. "I'm more than happy to entertain guests and constituents at any hour. I'm always here for you."

Fiss'Q smiled, nodding to them both to take a seat in her salon. Around them were the artifacts and trophies of Fiss'Q's career as both a Senator of Arokhnai, and as a swordswoman—gilded screens inset with watercolors of distant shores, a golden Mandrian helmet, polished to a high sheen, a dozen short blackwood spears wielded by the Massala warrior priests of the Golden City of Salmaria, several Unhuman sabers, an intricate Imperian blackwood clock, a Justiciar shield of white and blue, a Slaver City bullwhip, and three red-orange dragon teeth, mounted on bronzewood and amberwood stands.

"As it happens, I know who you are," Fiss'Q said. "You're a performer, yes?"

"I am," Lyra said.

"By your attire, I'd say you are the Black Bard of Valdikan," Fiss'Q said. "Correct?"

"The one and only, my lady," Lyra said, giving a little bow with a courtly flourish.

Fiss'Q gestured to An'Alta.

"Fetch some bloodwine and cheese for my guests, please, An'Alta," Fiss'Q said. "So, you are in danger, I take it?"

Kaden whipped his head around instinctively, prompting a smile from Fiss'Q.

"I'm being pursued," Lyra said. "I'm really quite sure of it."

"You're quite safe here," Fiss'Q said. "For now. But I must know *why* you are being pursued, if I am to protect you."

Lyra glanced at the luthier, and at the Senator, while An'Alta brought out a dark green crystal decanter of bloodwine and three cups, as well as a wheel of bone-white cheese, accompanied by darkbread, cut into a cluster of wedged slices, arrayed like a flower.

"How did you know we were in danger?" Kaden asked. His voice was raspy, his manner, fearful and nervous.

"On account of the Night's Violin, naturally," Fiss'Q said. "Which, I presume, you brought."

"I did," Lyra said, gesturing to the black leather case that she carried. She clutched it close to her chest. Fiss'Q admired the Sylvan workmanship of the case, itself, which looked both sturdy and delicate at the same time, elegant and functional at once.

"Let me see it, if I may," Fiss'Q said.

Lyra glanced at the luthier, as if by an unspoken bond between them, and set the case on the divan, unclasping it. Within the case was a bed of blue velvet. And, upon the blue velvet was the Night's Violin.

Lyra removed it, and Fiss'Q gasped at the sight of the lovely thing. It was glossy black. Sturdy, well-lacquered blackwood made up its body, while its strings were silver, standing out against the endless shade of the instrument's ebony fingerboard. There were tiny, lacquered runes drawn or etched around its edges, and the tuning pegs were matte blackwood. Its bridge looked to be carved from silverwood.

"Stunning," Fiss'Q said. She had heard about the legendary Sylvan instrument, thought lost generations ago, only recently reappearing at Valdikan, under most curious circumstances. "Can you play it for me?"

A trace of pride—not wounded, but present, nonetheless, played on Lyra's young face.

"Why, of course I can play it, my lady," Lyra said.

"Oh, I'm no lady," Fiss'Q said. "Not a noble, at any rate. I'm simply one senator among many in Arokhnai."

"Apologies, Senator. She's not from here, you know, isn't used to our ways," Kaden said, while Lyra drew forth the bow, which was made of the same blackwood at the Night's Violin, with ivory horsehair that was rumored to have been taken from the mane of a unicorn. True or not, Fiss'Q liked that bit of folklore surrounding the Violin.

"The Sylvanni made the Night's Violin, didn't they?" Fiss'Q asked. She knew that already, but was curious what Lyra knew of its provenance.

The mention of the Sylvans gave Lyra pause—the hint of something passing on her pretty face that Fiss'Q noted. Kaden spoke up, while Lyra composed herself.

"Yes, Senator," Kaden said. "The instrument is of Sylvan artifice. Miss Longbow came to ask me if I'd ever seen anything like it before, and, of course, I hadn't. It's a flawless instrument, and, well, being made of blackwood, is far stronger than it looks. Blackwood is a most curious choice on the part of the Sylvanni. Only *they* would have the skill to make a violin like that, although I've made my share of fine instruments over the years."

Fiss'Q had no doubt of that. Sylvan artisans were among the very greatest in the world. Anything they touched was made beautiful and wondrous by their artifice. Fiss'Q her-

self had Sylvan glasswork in one of her cabinets, glasses she brought out when she sought to impress honored guests.

"You must tell me how you came upon this wondrous instrument," Fiss'Q said, while Lyra drew the violin to her chin and sounded a haunting note with the bow. Fiss'Q could feel the instrument's power even in that simplest of gestures. As a Shadowlander, she could see far beyond the range of normal sight, and the instrument radiated magic above and beyond anything she'd ever seen.

Lyra began to play a strange and mournful tune, and Fiss'Q found herself transported, seeing and feeling Lyra's journey through Old Soria, in the company of a Sylvan caravan in the Free League, away from the looming threat of war, away from cities and civilization, itself. What a journey it had been, amid the ancient trees and lost Sorian ruins. The vistas were profoundly moving, whether the ironwood trees cracking apart the broken stone of lost temples to long dead gods, or defiant carved edifices that reveled in the studied, hubristic decadence of the Sorians, themselves.

Fiss'Q did not recognize the Sylvanni she saw in her vision, but their faces bore the enigmatic beauty that was their birthright, that blend of blithe longevity, matchless intrigue and cunning that defined all of their people. In the vision, they appeared to be merchant-warriors in the manner of their dress—the colored silks and delicately wrought armor, the slim Sylvan blades that could nonetheless pierce the strongest steel.

"You kept rare company," Fiss'Q said, when Lyra stopped playing.

"I did," Lyra said. "I was entrusted with the Night's Violin, but not by the Sylvanni."

Fiss'Q knew the Sylvanni well enough that they would not part with such a treasure without having weighed the cost of doing so very carefully. The Sylvanni lived far in the chilly north, in the twin realms of Solaria and Sylvannia. Nothing passed freely into the hands of Man from the Sylvanni without a price. In fact, for Fiss'Q, the presence of the instrument itself was portentous. And she was not, by her nature, one given over to portents.

"Who entrusted it to you?" Fiss'Q asked.

"The wizard, Farro, of Valdikan," Lyra said. "Although Lord Fallryn Bluewater of Solaria, Seneschal of the Archduke of Solaria, escorted me for a time, once it had been given to me. For my own protection, you see."

Fiss'Q glanced at Kaden, who looked on, enraptured at the mention of the Sylvanni nobility, still spellbound by the notes the Black Bard had played. For a dweller in the distant south, Sylvannia was a magical land, a place of mystery and wonder. And the Night's Violin possessed an exquisite and unique tone, far beyond anything even the most skilled of human luthiers could have created.

For Fiss'Q, it was something else. Alone of the people of Irth, the Sylvanni had endured. Even the mighty Sorians had risen and fallen without ever conquering them. They were not a people to give anything up freely.

Lyra looked searchingly at Fiss'Q, and at the luthier. The young woman was a troubadour, a wandering minstrel, of great repute in her persona as the Black Bard, Daughter to Darkness. Her mournful style had caught on in some of the noble merchant houses of the Leaguist Cities in the

Midlands—the city-states of the Free League held both frolic and sorrow dear to them.

Lyra Longbow had made a name for herself in this role, serving up sonorous sorrow on a silver platter for the merchant princes of the Leaguist cities. As the heirs and stewards of boundless good fortune, the Leaguists could safely wallow in woe and draw the most marvelous melancholy from it. For other, less fortunate places, the spectacle would have been too much to bear. For the Leaguists, it was something of a sport, this courting of sorrow amid a field of plenty.

"It is quite a gift," Fiss'Q said.

"Of course it is," Lyra said. "Well-earned, I must add."

"At what price?" Fiss'Q asked. Again, she knew the Sylvanni far too well to assume it was a gift given without hefty strings attached. How Lyra had managed to secure a Sylvan escort was itself a story the needed telling.

"That is between Lord Fallryn and myself, Senator," Lyra said, putting the instrument away, carefully wrapping it in blue velvet.

Kaden was sampling some of the bloodwine and cheese, tasting them before replying.

"You will protect us, Senator?" Kaden asked. "I fear that we are at risk on account of the instrument appearing in our city."

"As much as I am able," Fiss'Q replied. "But, if I am to protect you, I must know what Farro and Fallryn's intent was, delivering such an instrument into Lyra's possession."

Three

Barvikh and Darha had sequestered the warriors to a nearby dwelling, where they would be less conspicuous, while the two of them had stationed themselves outside Senator Fiss'Q's residence.

"If she's sheltered with Senator Fiss'Q, there's precious little we can do about it," Darha said. Barvikh was well-enough acquainted with the tangled politics of Arokhnai to understand that the house of a Senator was sacrosanct.

"We should just storm in tonight and take the bloody thing," Barvikh said. "Shadowlander or not, she's only one woman. My men could prevail against her."

Darha scoffed, looked at him like he had said something so utterly idiotic that she could scarcely contain her contempt. Her silver eyes flicked over him, incendiary in their appraisal.

"What?" Barvikh asked. "I'm not wrong."

"You are wrong beyond imagining," Darha said. "Fiss'Q would cut your men to bits before they knew what was happening. You've never faced a Shadowlander before, clearly."

Barvikh's pride was dented by her blunt assessment. True or not, it bothered him. Obsidiander corsairs were renowned for their fearlessness, their ruthlessness, and their brutality. They saw themselves not as men, but as forces of human nature, itself.

"And *you* have?" Barvikh asked.

"Yes," Darha said. "I have."

"Liar," Barvikh said. "Shadowmancer or not, I don't believe you."

The street was, like all of the elite districts of Arokhnai, quiet and peaceful. The fragrant swaywood trees that graced its avenues were well-tended and impeccably placed, offering comforting shade from the tyranny of the Southland sun. Down here, the heat was itself ever-present, and city dwellers had come up with their ways of dealing with it.

In lovely Arokhnai, it had been the conscientious cultivation of trees, gardens, and parks. Darha appreciated the artful attention to municipal beauty in this city. How unlike industrious Uriokh, or her home city of Ansible.

While Barikh had no doubt that Darha had come across all manner of adversaries, he found it hard to believe she'd contended with a Shadowlander.

"Did you prevail? Against the Shadowlander?" Barvikh asked.

"What do you think?" Darha asked. "I wouldn't be here if I hadn't."

Her silver-eyed gaze said much to the mercenary, if only by implication. She had not, of course, faced a Shadowlander before. But Darha had read a great deal about them in her study of Shadowmancy, and felt she knew them, if only from afar.

"So, what are we to do?" Barvikh asked.

"We wait until tonight," Darha said. "And then we strike."

"Wouldn't now be a better time to attack?" Barvikh asked. Not that he wanted to gainsay Darha, but to his mind, Shadowlanders were deadlier when more shadows were about. In the light of the day, they were, at least in theory, more vulnerable. It was the sort of workmanlike appraisal that was well-suited to a man of Uriokh.

Darha bored into him with her unnatural eyes, chilling him to his core.

"Yes," she said. "But the City Guard would respond, were we to attack her now. Better to wait until nightfall, so we only have Fiss'Q to contend with."

Barvikh watched wagons pass, bearing loads of blood oranges and other produce items. Arokhnai, despite its perilous position at the edge of desolate Southland swamps and on a routinely storm-tossed coast, was well-fed by her trade caravans.

"We only need to steal the Night's Violin," Darha said. "That's all we are here for, Barvikh. We are not here to try to slay the Senator."

"So you say, so you say," Barvikh replied. "What of the Black Bard?"

"What of her?" Darha asked. "Have your way with her. Enslave her. I don't care."

It wasn't a concession, and yet felt like one. Barvikh wanted to take the Black Bard for his own, have her sing her sorrowful songs for his pleasure, mourning her fate. He would bring her to Uriokh to sing tales of lamentation like a songbird. His father would love that. The Black Bard of Valdikan, laid low and enslaved in Uriokh for the rest of her days. Or, perhaps they'd trade her to the Manticore, for a hefty price. Barvikh's piratical mind navigated all the possibilities.

"When my father's war fleet arrives and Arokhnai's taken, I'll have her sing a song of its fall," Barvikh said. In his mind, he longed to see the proud republic's ruin. His father would see the pretty streets ploughed over, sown with salt. Or, perhaps better still, flooded and returned to the swamp that spawned this place, fed to the flies, snakes, and crocodilians that swarmed its shores. The creatures would feast on the dead of Arokhnai.

"If the prize is not recovered in time, Arokhnai will sink your precious fleet," Darha said. "And the Black Bard will sing of *your* demise, although you will not hear it, because you will be dead, Prince Barvikh."

"For *your* sake, that had better not come to pass," Barvikh said.

Barvikh glowered at the woman. Sorceress or not, no one talked to an Abbasa like that with impunity. It was only out of a healthy respect—he would not call it fear—for her skills as a magus that he stayed his hand. His father had given him orders to slit her throat once the Violin was acquired, and he was more than happy to carry out that directive.

"The Obsidian Fleet will not be sunk by Arokhnai," Barvikh said. "They do not even know we are coming for them. We will crucify the Shadowlanders, driving silver spikes through their hands and lining the walls of their fallen city with them, so they can spend eternity boiling in the sun. And we will let them watch us tear their city apart, enslaving her people. Its ruination will be absolute."

Darha smiled to herself. The man was such a blustering fool, like all the cocksure corsairs of Uriokh. Their insularity on their lovely island had given them pretensions toward assuming leadership among all of the Slaver Cities.

As a native of Ansible, she viewed things through a different lens. The City of Sorcerers saw Uriokh as a nothing more than a pretender to the throne of lost Soria. Ansible, at least, knew its place in the cosmic order of things.

"Uriokh is destined to rule the Southlands," Barvikh said. "My father has worked hard to make it so."

She had only taken the job offered by Korg Abbasa when she'd detected the Night's Violin in Arokhnai. After the incident at Valdikan the year before had caught her eye, Darha had woven spells to help her track the Violin, or at least when it was used.

Darha did not care about the destiny of Uriokh. Let the fool Obsidianders try to sink the city as they intended. In the chaos of war, she would, with the Night's Violin in hand, travel back to Ansible and earn her place among the most storied of magi. She would have her own tower, and would join the elders of Ansible. Or, better yet, she'd conquer the city for herself, becoming the Sorcerer-Queen of Ansible. That would enrage the Wizards Militant of Ansible beyond measure, and the thought gave Darha great pleasure.

"It's nice to have dreams," Darha said. Barvikh could hear the mockery in her tone and bristled at it. Silver-eyed sorceress or not, he would not be made sport of. Let her mock him when she was choking on her own blood.

"You would do well to remember that my father hired you," Barvikh said. "You are in our employ, not the other way around."

Darha pried her silver eyes from the Senator's residence to bore into the warrior prince, and, despite his bluster, he'd felt that familiar fear flex within him. It was no small thing to face down a sorcerer of Ansible. They were a fearsome folk who, Barvikh told himself, would one day fall to Uriokh as well, when the time was right. The pyres would burn for days, all of the wizards thrown upon them by the warriors of Uriokh. It would be a spectacle the Black Bard would sing for him, one day.

There were no native sorcerers on the Obsidian Island, although there was trade with them in the city of Forlarin on the eastern part of the island, near the twin volcanoes—Mortis and Vertis—that rumbled menacingly.

Magi would come to Forlarin for the obsidian that was the island's namesake, and to travel to the volcanoes, themselves, for arcane and, no doubt, sinister purposes. Most avoided the terrifying volcanoes, which routinely erupted, filling the sky with their sulfurous clouds. Only sorcerers would be mad enough to frequent them.

"We are all slaves to our passions," Darha said.

"I am no slave," Barvikh said.

"But you could be," Darha said. "With a snap of my finger, I could bind you to me, for as long as I liked."

As if to prove her point, she held up a slender hand, opalescent fingernails poised as she snapped her finger once. He could see that she had a black rune carefully painted on each gleaming fingernail. As before, he could feel the powerful magic about her, pressing on him in unfamiliar and unwelcome ways.

"I am not your enemy, enchantress," Barvikh said. "The Shadowlander is."

"And I am not your slave, Prince," Darha said. "But you could be mine. Do well to remember this."

Her magician's hand remained as she left it, hovering motionless, like a threat. If his men had been with him, Barvikh would have made more of a show of things, to

illustrate his contempt for the sorceress. As it was just the two of them, and he could not be sure that her threat was not genuine, Barvikh relented.

"You have nothing to worry about from me, Darha," Barvikh said, watching her slowly bring her hand down. He consoled himself to imagine those lovely hands in manacles. Her time would come, as surely as it would for the Shadowlander, and Arokhnai. After the fall of the city, rather than slitting her throat, he'd clap her in irons and she'd adorn his villa as a prize in Uriokh, along with the Black Bard.

She studied him in silence a moment, before turning her penetrating gaze back to the residence of Fiss'Q.

"We'll strike tonight," Darha said. "When the moon rises."

Four

Lyra, performer that she was, seemed ready to tell her tale. She reassured Kaden with a glance before speaking, while Fiss'Q looked on.

"Born in Hightower, I was used to performing through-out the Leaguist Cities," Lyra said. "They are all, as you know, eager for entertainments and possess plentiful coin to spend. And, with the Manticore marching with his armies, I daresay I feel that people are desirous of distrac-tion. Even of a sort that I may bring."

Fiss'Q, like anyone acquainted with the goings on in Irth, and more than most, understood the menace posed by the monstrous Manticore. Although no one knew for sure who he was, Fiss'Q suspected he had once been a Southland sorcerer, who had managed to acquire some of Old Soria's darkest secrets to transform himself.

He took that sliver of blood magical power he'd ac-quired and headed east decades ago, where he'd impressed a horde of Unhuman horsemen, and had promptly put them to work going to war with the cities of Man, starting in the icy north of the Justiciar Lands. There, the pious and fanatical warrior-knights fell before him, followed by the fractious Border Kingdom of Conradia to the west.

After that, the Manticore had traveled south to harass the Free League cities, where, thankfully, the art of war was more advanced, and his advancement had slowed. But the threat he posed was profound, and not lost to the Republic of Arokhnai. The Manticore was insatiable in his drive for conquest.

"I was in Valdikan," Lyra said. "The Magical City. I had performed 'The Song of the Lost Sorrow' at the behest of the wizard, Farro of Nightside, in his hall, before his friends and allies."

The "Song of Lost Sorrow" was an epic poem of considerable length, a great lyrical mountain to climb for any minstrel. That Lyra had performed it showed her considerable confidence as a performer. And in front of the war wizard, Farro, no less. He was a mercenary magus, lending his services where required, and was doubtless being paid very well by Valdikan to help keep the Manticore at bay.

"What's Farro like?" Fiss'Q asked. She knew of the man, but had never met him. Lyra seemed both amused at the question and bemused at the interruption of her story.

"Like all magi, to be truthful, Senator," Lyra said. "Brash, full of himself. Confident to the point of arrogance, and, yet, tinged with a curious vulnerability, as if all of his arcane explorations may be for naught, in the end."

Lyra's speaking voice was lovely to hear, and the young woman's charm radiated out from her, despite her funereal attire. Most bards adopted more brightly-colored or festive raiment, but the Black Bard's eschewal of those things had made her quite distinctive among her peers.

"He commissioned that I perform the poem for him and his friends," Lyra said. "Among them was Lord Fallryn Bluewater, and his retinue."

Fiss'Q thought about that a moment, and then a moment more. That Farro had an association with the Sylvanni was curious.

"Unusual to see a military magus like Farro consorting with the Sylvanni," Fiss'Q said. "And vice versa."

The Sylvanni were notoriously untrustworthy and capricious in their dealings, and seldom involved ever themselves in matters of Man. They sent forth their trade caravans from Sylvannia and Solaria, their twin realms, for purposes of both trade and the gathering of information.

"Quite so," Lyra said, clearly unused to being interrupted. "After my performance, I was invited to dine with Lord Fallryn and Farro, in the latter's banquet hall. As you must know in Valdikan, the Council Arcane runs that city, and Farro has been a member of said Council for decades—although, in truth, he does not look his age. I would not put him long past his prime, to judge him on his appearance."

Along with more mundane pursuits such as turning lead into gold and soothsaying, rare was the magus who did not at least attempt immortality, or longevity, at the very least. It was one of their many obsessions, one that the Shadowlanders had themselves solved millennia before. Such was the plight of the magi, to still be trying to chase down these things that the rulers of Arokhnai had solved long, long ago.

"Lord Fallryn himself had been greatly moved by my performance," Lyra said. "He was, like all Sylvanni, beautiful—blue-haired and purple-eyed—the hallmarks of Sylvanni nobility, I'll have you know."

"Yes, I know," Fiss'Q said. All members of the Sylvan royal family had blue hair. The fairy-touched Sylvanni

all had the most beautiful hair of all sorts of hues. But the obligatory royal blue of the Sylvan blood royale was widely known. Although she did not know Lord Fallryn personally, as an aristocrat of Solaria and a warrior in the fey manner of the Sylvanni, she knew he was almost assuredly a proxy of the elusive Sylvan Faerie Queen, herself, conducting business on behalf of the Crown.

"I rather think he took a liking to me," Lyra said. "If you must know."

Fiss'Q only smiled, more to herself than to the young bard. Sylvanni were, in addition to being treacherous negotiators, rather rigorous in their amorous activities. Many was the human—and others—who had been seduced by a Sylvan. To be looked upon by a Sylvan was to feel loved by one. Whatever they truly felt, only the Sylvanni knew.

"I can understand why," Fiss'Q said. "You're quite charming, Lyra."

"Pardon me, Senator," Kaden said. "But I really should go back to my shop, as Miss Longbow's told me this story before. I wish you both the best of luck. And, should you ever need an instrument made, by all means, come to me."

Fiss'Q smiled and nodded, shaking the luthier's hand as he rose. Lyra was particularly put out to have her story so interrupted, and rose as well, her grey eyes flashing.

"Thank you for guiding me to the Senator's residence, Kaden," Lyra said. "I never forget a favor."

Kaden nodded and smiled, and Fiss'Q had An'Alta show him to the door. When he was gone, Fiss'Q and Lyra returned to where they were, after Fiss'Q poured some more wine. The Black Bard continued her story.

"Thank you, Senator," Lyra said, taking the cup of wine and drinking deep of it. "As you may also know, the Manticore had sent some of his army to attempt to take Valdikan. The city war wizards had applied themselves to the defense of the city, and had been fairly successful in keeping the Unhumans at bay. For all their savagery on the battlefield, the Unhumans are terrified of magic."

"Indeed," Fiss'Q said. "They have reason to be. They themselves suffered mightily under the scaled hands of the Sorians and their blood magic, long ago. The Sorians created them as warrior-slaves, and they have not forgotten this."

Lyra nodded, again piqued that Fiss'Q was even speaking up. The child did not understand that a Senator of Arokhnai was duty-bound to speak early and often, as was a necessary adjunct of their station in the Republic of Arokhnai. A silent Senator was a powerless and inconsequential one. No one would ever accuse Fiss'Q of being inconsequential, at least not to her face.

"At any rate," Lyra said. "After the meal, Farro revealed the Night's Violin to me, as payment for my performance of the poem. 'You have performed admirably tonight, Lyra,' he said. 'It is only fitting that I reward you accordingly.'"

"Quite a gift," Fiss'Q said. And it was. The value of the instrument was inestimable.

"It most certainly was," Lyra said. "I was humbled by it. Admittedly, my performance of the poem had been immaculate. Everyone knows how good I am with words and song. But to be gifted the Night's Violin? It was beyond anything I could have imagined. And Farro was gracious about it, in his sorcerous way. 'I hope you are able to make

music with this as beautiful as the music you made for us tonight' he said."

Lyra paused to take another drink of bloodwine before continuing, and Fiss'Q waited patiently. Had Farro intended to give it to Fallryn, but, for reasons only he knew, gifted it to Lyra, instead? Or was it some scheme the two men had worked out in advance? Fiss'Q was suspicious. As wonderful as her verse may have been, to have paid her with the Night's Violin was payment far beyond her artful achievement.

"'The Manticore's army will reach Valdikan within days,' Lord Fallryn said. 'We can spirit the Night's Violin away, Farro.' I could tell from the way he said it that he intended for *me* to be spirited away, as well. And, to be honest, I was prepared for this. I had never been privileged to travel with the Sylvanni before. I welcomed the opportunity."

Fiss'Q smiled, her little fangs dancing on her lower lip as she did so. A Sylvanni caravan would have been the last place Fiss'Q would want to be. But, for a young bard, it would have been a wonderful chance for a memorable glimpse into another world.

"Farro, however, would hear none of it," Lyra said. "Instead, he encouraged me to take up the Night's Violin for the defense of Valdikan. 'Now is not the time to flee, Lord Fallryn,' Farro said. 'But to fight. I have given the Black Bard the weapon she needs to protect the city.' Fallryn looked at him and said 'It cannot be so desperate a need as this, can it, Lord Farro? She will be marked by the Manticore, should she use this instrument in this fashion.' Now, you must know that my curiosity was more than piqued by this cryptic exchange between these powerful men. I

am simply an entertainer—I tell stories, I sing songs, I play instruments—I'm not some warrior queen."

"It's difficult to be a warrior queen," Fiss'Q said. "It's even difficult being a warrior senator, to be truthful."

Fiss'Q's little joke was, at best, mildly received by the young bard, who continued with her story, after taking a moment to sample more of the bloodwine, while An'Alta hovered in the shadows.

"I asked the men, 'What would you have me do?' I am the first to say that I have no love for the Manticore, or his Unhuman legions. If I could, in some small way, lend a hand, I would. It was Farro who spoke, and with great solemnity. 'In three days, the warlord Grokthar will be at the gates of Valdikan with one hundred thousand Unhuman horsemen. There will be siege towers and other weapons of war. The War Wizards are assembled, and we shall defend Valdikan to the last man and woman. But we fear that, despite our efforts, the Manticore and his legions could break through. Rather, we need to make a stand. You can help us with this, using the Night's Violin.'"

Fiss'Q knew the stories of the instrument. It was said to be possessed of almost limitless magical power.

But only if was able to play it. Any false note struck could have the most dire of consequences for the user. In this way, a great fear of the instrument had grown up around it—stories of less than stellar players turning themselves to stone, for example. Or one unfortunate thief who found himself literally fading out of existence before the stunned eyes of onlookers. The Night's Violin exacted the heaviest of tolls upon those who dared to abuse it.

"So, you see that I was taken aback by the suggestion that I might be able to protect the people of Valdikan—

itself a lovely city in its own right, although it pales before the ancient majesty of Arokhnai, Senator, I assure you," Lyra said.

Fiss'Q smiled to herself again at this young woman's attempt to appeal to the civic pride of citizens of Arokhnai. Anyone living there knew the city-state to be the pearl of the Sorian Sea, despite the imperial pretensions of her Slaver City rivals.

"Yes, Valdikan possesses its own sort of Northlandish…charm," Fiss'Q said, pleased that Lyra seemed to appreciate her quip.

"I told the men that I would do whatever was required of me," Lyra said. "And Farro was gratified by this. He said 'The Night's Violin possesses a great magic that only a master musician can call forth. Magic that can win the day. Are you up to this lofty task, Lyra?' To hear Farro speak to me this way, I was so honored. That I, and I alone, could save an entire city? It was incredible to contemplate, although Lord Fallryn took me aside and expressed reservations. I tell you this: when a Sylvan gazes upon you with concern in their eyes, it gives a person pause. 'Young Lyra, I fear the wizard Farro asks too much of you in this endeavor,' he said. 'You should leave Valdikan to her war wizards, you should not involve yourself in this war. You are a performer and a musician. Leave war to the warriors.' I could hear the sincerity in his voice, could see the earnestness in his eyes, Senator. He was persuasive. And, yet, I could not abandon magical Valdikan in her time of need. 'I can't do this, Lord Fallryn,' I said. 'I must remain to defend her from the Manticore, as only I can.' And Fallryn continued, anyway. 'Understand this, then: should you raise a hand against the Manticore, you will

be his enemy for life. Should you take this stand at Valdikan, he will never stop until he kills you.' I could see the concern he had for me, Senator. His elegant and beautiful features betrayed such effortless, gracious sincerity. A teller of mournful tales I may be, but my heart was moved by his honorable concern for my well-being. I wanted to flee with him that very night, wherever he would take me. But my own sense of duty prevailed, and, I'll admit, a desire to perform a miracle. 'Thank you for your concern, My Lord,' I said. 'However, I cannot abandon this city. Even if I am damned by the Manticore.' He accepted this, with a trace of sadness about his serene face—and that whisper of sorrow almost broke me, Senator. 'Then, I will remain in the city,' Fallryn said. 'To take you from this place after the deed is done. For there is another matter you must consider—should you succeed in performing the task at hand, the wizards of Valdikan will not want you to leave. They will seek to keep you here. And, I can tell that you are not the sort of woman who would be kept in this fashion.' He was right, of course. I am no prisoner, Senator. I will not be imprisoned."

Lyra watched An'Alta light candles in the room, one by one, the young woman attending to her duties with her characteristic solemnity, while Fiss'Q knew she'd been eavesdropping on them the whole time. Such was her nature.

"So," Fiss'Q said. "The Manticore's army arrived...."

"Yes," Lyra said. "Three days, just as Farro had foretold. And, Senator, I would say to you that they were the most terrifying thing I've ever seen. A grey sea of armored Unhumans, bearing pikes and spears, axes, and cruelly curved swords. This horrifying army, with their renowned cavalry, the grey warhorses, pawing the ground with their

thundering hooves. I've never been to war, Senator, and seeing this legion at the gates of Valdikan put the fear in me. And all of them riding under the banner of the Manticore—the pink and gold of that cursed standard, in mocking contrast to the sternly redoubtable Unhumans. On that day, Senator, the sky was cloudy, but the clouds themselves were like a sea of grey—a lighter grey than the claylike Unhumans, who glowered at us with their blood-red eyes and fanged mouths, who beat a cacophonous rhythm on their shields with their sabers, bellowing curses at us, egged on by their leaders. Grokthar himself, a high lieutenant of the Manticore, presided at the head of his army, wearing the most curious golden armor, emblazoned with the Manticore's standard, the upraised paw, rampant. He roared a threat to us, to throw open our gates before the army tore them down. Despite the bravado of the war wizards, the citizen-soldiers of Valdikan were afraid. I was terrified, even when Farro took me to the wall and said to me 'Child, you must play, now. Walk along the walls with the Night's Violin beneath your chin and play like your life depended upon it. You must play, or we shall all die.' And, Senator, I was afraid. 'What song should I play?' I asked. I have played a number of instruments in my young life, Senator, but I had never played so fine an instrument as this violin I held in my hands. Farro sighed, and looked me in the eye. 'Play from your heart, and play for your life,' Farro said. 'You will know the tune.'"

Lyra finished her cup of wine, and An'Alta, pausing from her candle-lighting, made a move to refill her cup, but Fiss'Q waved her off, poured more for Lyra.

"What song did you play?" Fiss'Q asked.

"I played 'The Sea of Trees' by the Sylvanni musician-poet Talerein," Lyra said. "And I walked along the battlements of Valdikan, playing that tune upon the Night's Violin, stepping my way, the fear of falling as much in my head as my fear of the Unhuman army, itself, who bellowed at me and brandished their weapons—mercifully, they were some distance from Valdikan's walls, out of the range of the city's archers, though not out of range of the Violin, which sounded with a force borne of its thrumming silver strings. But, because the Unhumans wielded these monstrous longbows—yes, I'm aware of the significance relative to my surname, Senator—they were able to fire upon me. So, imagine this—I'm playing the Night's Violin along the battlements of Valdikan, while Unhuman arrows fly at me like angry bees. As I played and minded my step, I imagined those deadly arrows turning into flowers, and wouldn't you know it, as the arrows flew, they turned to black roses as they neared me. In their bid to kill me, the Unhumans had accidentally treated the city of Valdikan to a shower of roses, to the terrified delight of the citizens. Grokthar, however, was not delighted by this. Rather, he brayed out an order to his troops, and a dozen monstrous horns sounded, and the army began marching on the city. The siege engines rolled forward, and the Unhuman archers continued with their assault of roses. More than a few of them struck me, those roses, I'll have you know, Senator. But I was emboldened. I walked back and forth along the walls of Valdikan, playing the Night's Violin with greater fervor than before, and as I performed, as those silver strings of the instrument vibrated beneath that whirring bow, as I looked out at the world across the lacquered field of the instrument itself, to the grey sea of

evil beyond me, I felt the power of the thing, the presence of it touch my spirit, like a muse. 'What would you have me do?' I felt it ask of me, and the desire make Grokthar's army go away, to take away the ugliness of this war and replace it with something beautiful, and in that moment, something flew from me to the Unhuman army, and they began to howl and scream in terror."

Lyra paused, taking another drink of the bloodwine, while An'Alta waited by another clutch of candles, looking on with big eyes. Fiss'Q leaned forward, fascination dancing on her own face.

"The Unhumans, starting with the ones within earshot, became a thicket of thorns," Lyra said. "I had turned them all into a forest of roses, before the eyes of everyone. They became a twisted tangle of thorns, dense and impassable, and where the siege towers stood, they became great hearthwood trees. The whole army became afflicted, transforming into a sea of black roses with grey stems and light silver thorns. And shiny Grokthar, himself, became a goldenwood tree in the middle of the massive thicket. I played the song until there was no army left on the battlefield. Some of the Unhumans, the ones at the back of the besieging army, had fled in horror from the spectacle. But most of them had become this mass of flowers gathered at the very eastern gates of Valdikan. When the deed was done and the song was ended, I paused and basked in the ecstatic cheers that went up from the walls of Valdikan. Even the war wizards applauded me, and Farro himself praised my miraculous performance. I was humbled and honored and stepped down from the battlements, to the waiting arms of the soldiers who had been ready to give their lives that day, and was hailed as the savior of the city.

'I knew you could do it,' Farro said. 'Marvelous performance, young Lyra.' And I was both proud and afraid in that moment. What else could I be?"

Fiss'Q had heard rumors of the miraculous setback for the Manticore at Valdikan, but, as with such rumors of war, one could not be sure just what to believe, especially a story as incredible as this.

An'Alta slipped away silently, as was her way, leaving the two of them in the room. Fiss'Q had no doubt she would still be listening, but the mousy young woman made it her business to be as unobtrusive as she could be.

"So, what happened after that?" Fiss'Q asked.

"I fled Valdikan," Lyra said. "Just as Fallryn had planned. After having words with Farro, Fallryn and his entourage spirited me away on their trade caravan, before the wizards could compel me to become Valdikan's poetic protector-in-residence. In the company of the Sylvanni, I was guarded from the scrying of the sorcerers, and able to pass from the city undetected. 'You have won the day,' Fallryn said. 'But the Manticore will know of the Black Bard, now, and what she has wrought. You will never know another night of peace.' In that moment, with the Night's Violin in hand, I could hardly care. I'd saved Valdikan. Women and children had gathered up all of those arrow-born black roses in the city and handed them out to the soldiers, who pinned them to their uniforms. I'd even taken one or two for myself. The massive bramble along the east gate of Valdikan was left undisturbed, an impassable monument to the battle, a sea of black roses, a cluster of hearthwood trees, and that lone goldenwood tree, its arms upraised. The people of Valdikan began at once telling the stories of the Black Bard of Valdikan, who had walked upon the ramparts and turned the Manticore's mightiest army into a sea of roses. Another bard, a rival of mine, if you must know—Janni the Whisperer—made a song about it: 'The Black Roses of Valdikan' and the man has wined and dined on that song for the better part of a year, while I'm in hiding for my very life. What justice is there in that, I ask you, Senator?"

Fiss'Q's private smile became more expansive, and she nodded. She was going to say something more when they were attacked.

Five

For a moment, it was just Fiss'Q and her guest, and a moment later, there appeared within the room a dozen Obsidianders, accompanied by a black-robed and silver-eyed woman of venomous smile and sorcerous bearing.

The men bore spears and swords, and rushed at Fiss'Q, who grabbed Lyra and the Night's Violin.

"Get it!" the sorceress said, pointing to the Night's Violin, and the Obsidianders lunged for Fiss'Q, who parted the Veil, her hand in Lyra's, and her other hand on the leathern case of the violin.

As a Shadowlander, Fiss'Q could commune with the Shadowlands themselves, a parallel realm that was the domain of the Prince of Shadows, one of the oldest of gods of Irth. In this place, beyond the Veil, the world of Man was represented as a ghostly version of itself. Normally, when a Shadowlander passed beyond the Veil, they could not be seen by the gaze of anyone rooted in the material world.

However, the silver-eyed sorceress was gazing right at them. Fiss'Q had never had someone able to gaze at her from beyond the Veil before, and it alarmed her.

"She's there," the woman said, ordering some of the men about, who ran around, uncertain. They could not touch

Fiss'Q or Lyra, because they were not truly there. And only the sorceress could see them.

"Here," Fiss'Q said. "Take your instrument."

Lyra was stunned to be in the Land of Shadow, and Fiss'Q could see great waves of fear and other emotion rolling off of her. This was no place for a mortal, Fiss'Q knew.

"It's beautiful," Lyra said. "And frightening, beyond imagining."

The Obsidianders ran about trying to locate Fiss'Q, while some of the others of them had taken An'Alta.

"Come back, Senator," the sorceress said. "Or the girl dies."

The emotion continued to boil off of Lyra, for her contact with Fiss'Q meant that she could hear what Fiss'Q heard, and see what she might see. Fiss'Q could see An'Alta's fear and trusting confidence that Fiss'Q would not abandon her. Fiss'Q would not betray that trust.

Fiss'Q backed away from the room, seeming to float, toward her favorite, nameless black blade, which was on display along the far wall. Two-handed, yet lean and swift, it was her most cherished weapon. The sorceress could see her looking at it, and barked orders to the warriors to grab the greatsword.

Even though she could see them, Fiss'Q knew that she moved quicker in the Shadowlands, and would be able to snag the weapon before they could reach it. In fact, she did, snatching up the sword. She slashed at the men with it, lancing up at them from the shadows they cast in the candlelight created by An'Alta when she'd lit the sconces.

The midnight sword cut through three, then four of the Obsidianders, and Lyra marveled at the men's auras flashing with pain and peril, as their spirits left them in their swift deaths, their bodies falling to the floor.

The sorceress had, along with the Obsidianders, committed a grievous offense in attacking Fiss'Q this way. The Senator of Arokhnai would never let such an affront go unchallenged.

"Senator, if you do not desist, the girl dies," the woman said. "I mean it."

One of the warriors put a sword to the neck of An'Alta. Fiss'Q loved the girl, and would do anything to protect her.

"I can't let her die," Fiss'Q said. "But you can't give them the instrument. It's far too precious."

The sorceress appeared to be bringing forth another conjuration, and Fiss'Q thought about who this woman might be. She was young, with black hair and a coldly pretty sort of bearing that was made still more pronounced by those piercing silver eyes.

"Can you play a tune?" Fiss'Q asked.

"Not while you hold my hand," Lyra said.

"Of course not," Fiss'Q said. She could not let go of Lyra, not here, because doing so would cast her off in the Land of Shadow, and even Fiss'Q might find her difficult to find. "And you must not let go."

"Then what are we to do?" Lyra asked.

"There's little I can do while that woman is staring at us," Fiss'Q said. "Not while I carry you."

Lyra looked at her.

"Then let me go," Lyra said.

"Never," Fiss'Q said. "This is no place for you. I cannot abandon An'Alta. We must return. You can leave the Violin here."

"Never," Lyra said. "It goes where I go."

"We can recover it," Fiss'Q said. "It will be right here."

"No," Lyra said. "I will not part with it."

"Senator, you are killing your servant girl," the woman said. "Come back at once."

Where had this woman come from? Then it occurred to her.

"Ansible," Fiss'Q said, seeing the runes that glowed from the woman's fingernails. "You're a sorceress of Ansible."

"Very good, Senator," the woman said. "I am Darha Lonai. I am a Shadowmancer, as you have likely discovered. Come forth, so that we may negotiate in person. Or the girl dies. You know I'm here for the Violin."

"I'm not giving up the Violin," Lyra whispered to Fiss'Q. "Not for anyone or anything."

Shadowmancers were almost mythical, so few of them existed. Such was the peril of Shadowmancy. They had incantations that made them able to get at Shadowlanders, using dark magics pulled from the most ancient Sorian scrolls and books. It was not blood magic; it was something else, entirely. Something far older.

Fiss'Q parted the Veil and the two of them reappeared in the room, with as much distance between themselves and the Obsidianders as possible.

Darha Lonai seemed pleasantly surprised.

"Soft choice, Senator," Darha said. "I would have let Barvikh and his men kill the girl, had our positions been reversed."

Fiss'Q regarded the remaining Obsidianders, who looked on with fear-flecked aggression. A fight with a Shadowlander was never undertaken carelessly.

"The instrument," Darha said. "Give it to us."

Lyra shook her head. "It's mine. It was gifted to me."

The sorceress shook her head.

"I don't care how you came upon it," Darha said. "I want it."

The Obsidianders moved to flank Fiss'Q and Lyra, and Fiss'Q raised her black sword. It was not ideal in her home environment, as the blade required room to be effective. The warriors tensed.

"We seem to be at a stalemate," Fiss'Q said.

"Does it appear that way to you, Senator?" Darha asked. She gestured, her hands appearing to glow with an opalescent radiance, and the Night's Violin vanished from Lyra's hands in a burst of shadow, appearing in Darha's.

Lyra yelped at the theft, while Darha laughed.

"You see?" Darha said. Then she ran for the door with one of the men, while the Obsidianders threw themselves at Fiss'Q and Lyra. Fiss'Q could see that the men had silver-tipped spears, which meant that they could hurt her, and brought her sword up to defend herself against them.

"Behind me, Lyra," Fiss'Q said.

"I can fight," Lyra said, drawing her own rapier.

"Please don't," Fiss'Q said. "I need you to help me recover the Violin. An'Alta, as we have practiced, my dear."

Fiss'Q parted the Veil again and slipped out of reach of the Obsidianders, while An'Alta bit one of the men on his hand, fleeing into the townhome while the man was distracted. The girl knew of the secret rooms Fiss'Q had in her home, places where she might hide from the Obsidianders.

Lyra jabbed at some of the men with her rapier, acquitting herself well enough with the quick blade, holding the men off. Judging from her style, Fiss'Q thought she'd had a lesson or two in swordplay from Lord Fallryn.

The Shadowlander acted quickly, cutting at the men with her greatsword from the shelter of the shadows that they cast, the nameless blade slashing at them from their

feet, bringing them down. In moments, the men were dead, dying, or wounded on the floor, and Fiss'Q reappeared, but only for a moment, to speak to Lyra, who was shaken at the newly made bloodbath in the room.

"You stay here," Fiss'Q said. "I'm going to pursue Darha."

She then parted the Veil yet again, and set off in pursuit, flowing through the insubstantial walls. In the netherlight of the Shadowlands, the souls of Darha and the man who ran with her were bright and clear in the darkness of the ghost of Arokhnai, and Fiss'Q gave chase.

Darha glanced over her shoulder, her silver eyes flashing, and Fiss'Q could see that the sorceress had seen her, and was smiling.

Fiss'Q pursued, moving even faster than before.

Six

"She's coming for us," Darha said. "Your men did not last long against her."

"Long enough," Barvikh said, as they ran. "You have the prize."

"For now," Darha said, handing it to him. "You must hold onto it, for I'll need both my hands free if I'm to hold back the Shadowlander."

They ran through the Artisan Quarter, were making their way toward the docks. If all went as intended, they would reach their boat and be able to sail off before any alarm was sounded. But everything hinged on being able to stop the Shadowlander.

Darha felt a thrill at the opportunity for this battle. She'd spent years honing her craft in Ansible, learning the complex mechanics of Shadowmancy. Few sorcerers ever dared to explore this dangerous and arcane magic, but Darha had felt it was a way of distinguishing herself in Ansible, where there were already so many practitioners of other sorts of magic.

That, and she envied Arokhnai's privileged position among the Sorian cities. For too long, everyone had quaked before the feared Shadowlanders. Even powerful wizards would speak of them only when they were compelled to do so.

"Night of blight, vanish us from her sight," Darha said, exultant at the familiar flow of arcane energy through her body as the spell took hold and cast a protective globe around them, camouflaging their auras.

Fiss'Q saw it immediately, which is to say that she saw them wink out of view, their spirit trails snuffed out as if they had been candles. Cursing, she parted the Veil and brought herself back to the here and now, where she could see them again. She'd be more vulnerable and slower in the everyday world, but at least she could still see them.

The fact that she was dealing with a Shadowmancer worried her. Shadowmancy was itself a nearly lost school of magic that allowed magi the opportunity to access the Shadowlands. Most Shadowmancers ended up getting themselves killed, for the Land of Shadow was not a place that welcomed strangers. The apparent youth of Darha was something noteworthy to Fiss'Q, as it implied either great talent or great desperation on the part of the young woman to pursue Shadowmancy. Maybe both, in fact.

They appeared to be heading toward the docks. No doubt to a waiting vessel, to attempt to flee with the Violin.

Darha glanced over her shoulder to see Fiss'Q still pursuing them. The Shadowlander had, as expected, returned to this world, so she could see them. All as Darha had planned. In fact, everything was going as she had planned. And she had planned so carefully.

"Keep heading to the ship, no matter what happens here, Barvikh," Darha said. Barvikh, for once, actually listened to her, and kept running.

Then she called forth a shadowbow—which, in her pale hands looked like a curved line of black smoke with a radiant string that was nearly as iridescent as her rune-covered fingernails. She drew on the string and loosed a shadowy arrow at Fiss'Q.

Fiss'Q saw the shadow arrow fly at her, and dodged the first shot, only to cry out as the arrow turned around and struck her in the back of her shoulder. Governed by the will of the Shadowmancer, the arrow would fly where she wanted it to. And, being made of the same essence of darkness as she was, the arrow could harm her. The shadow arrow vanished as soon as it had struck her, leaving only a wound that bled indigo.

Pleased at the results of her efforts, Darha loosed three more shadow arrows at Fiss'Q, who struck at them with her black sword, cutting them as they reached her. Each cut turned them back into smoky shadow.

"Give it up, Senator," Darha said, grinning at her from behind the curve of her shadowbow. "The prize is mine. You've lost this one."

"If the arrows follow your direction," Fiss'Q said. "You could have killed me with your first shot."

"I really don't want to kill you, Senator," Darha said.

Fiss'Q knew she was only delaying her, while her confederate made off with the Night's Violin, but she could not leave the Shadowmancer alone, under the circumstances. The woman was a threat, and had to be dealt with.

"You're got some nice tricks, Darha," Fiss'Q said, circling her warily. "But Shadowmancy exacts a hefty toll on those who practice it. The Prince of Shadows notices when people steal from Him. He's the god of thieves."

The young sorceress sneered at her.

"And intrigue, conspiracy, and espionage. I know who He is. Let Him come," Darha said. "I welcome Him."

She loosed three more shadow arrows at Fiss'Q, who blocked one and was struck by two more, gasping as they found their marks—one on her thigh, the other in her other shoulder. Fiss'Q knew the girl was toying with her, although she did not know why. That angered her, and caused Fiss'Q to part the Veil and slip away from the here and now.

For in that moment, Fiss'Q knew that the young woman's pride had unmoored her. She had wanted to fight a Shadowlander too badly, to try out her Shadowmancy. But, as Fiss'Q darted into the Shadowlands, racing again toward the docks, she knew that the sorceress would not be able to get there before her, despite her craft.

Wounded though she was, Fiss'Q pressed on, while she was sure Darha followed hard in her wake, dismissing the shadowbow and running after her. Although Fiss'Q could not see her because of her incantation, she knew the Shadowmancer would be angry that Fiss'Q had broken off their fight that way. Loathe as Fiss'Q was to break off a fight, the recovery of the Night's Violin compelled it.

Seven

Lyra had headed to the docks after the attack on Fiss'Q's home. She would die before she lost the Night's Violin. She saw the Obsidiander warrior reach the ship, which, to her eyes, looked like a sleek, black-sailed Uriokh vessel. Not a warship galley, nor even a privateer, but a smuggler's sort of boat, designed for speed and stealth, rather than ostentation.

To her dismay, the vessel was already making its way to leave the harbor, slipping her ropes and sliding along the quay.

"No!" Lyra said, watching it go.

Then she saw Fiss'Q appear out of nowhere, rising like a wraith out of the shadows, to appear aboard the ship. She wanted to say something, but Fiss'Q was going about her business with her greatsword, slaying Obsidiander warriors, who mustered to try to stop her. From where Lyra stood, she could see the fight was escalating, as a bell was rung and more soldier-sailors of Uriokh ran to try to stop the Shadowlander.

Lyra brought out her second favorite stringed instrument—her crossbow, which she'd long ago named "Temperance"—a Hightower breechbow, and loaded it with a bolt. Although she could not vault across the quay to the fleeing ship, she could at least lend a hand by firing shots at the Obsidianders.

She loosed a bolt, pleased by the quiet twang of the crossbow, gratified that she felled an Obsidiander with it.

Fiss'Q vanished from view, lost in shadow, while Lyra fired again, and again. At this relatively close range, Temperance was devastating, and she took down two more warriors, who were running about, looking for Fiss'Q and trying to determine the source of the crossbow bolts.

"I have a quarrel with you, Obsidiander," Lyra said, softly to herself. "Or a quarrel *for* you, if you prefer."

Pleased with her pun, she fired another bolt, catching yet another man, tacking him to the mast by the throat, while he sputtered and died choking on his blood. The sailors had finally spotted Lyra, and were firing upon her with bows and arrows. The arrows thunked into the boxes around her, perilously close.

Lyra took shelter, reloaded Temperance, and waited for an opportunity to shoot. More arrows clattered about, seeking her.

Suddenly, Fiss'Q emerged from the shadows near her, holding the Night's Violin in its case. The Shadowlander was panting and splashed with indigo, giving Lyra an uneasy smile. Lyra could see that she was wounded, and that the indigo was her blood. Her own black sword was slick with bright red blood.

"Your instrument is recovered," Fiss'Q said. "We must get away from here at once. We are in considerable danger."

Lyra was overjoyed at the return of the Night's Violin, and set Temperance down, flipping open the case to gaze at the gorgeous instrument within. Even in the darkness on

the docks, amid the fusillade of arrows and the angry shouts of Obsidiander soldiers, the instrument comforted her.

"What are you doing?" Fiss'Q asked, catching her breath. "We must flee."

"Not just yet, Senator," Lyra said, plucking the violin with her fingertips, while readying the bow. She would have her revenge on these men who had attempted to rob her.

She began to play a tune, a fiery song that made the silver strings sing. Lyra turned and played the tune for the Obsidianders. It was not a song Fiss'Q had recognized, but as Lyra sawed with the bow, the anger that flared within her was plain to see. And the Night's Violin answered her anger in kind, the beautiful, baleful notes sounding, as the Obsidiander archers loosed arrows at the Black Bard. Musician and instrument danced together on the dock, and the Black Bard would not be denied, nor would the Night's Violin deny her.

As their arrows arced toward her, they burst into fleeting flame, lighting up the sky for moments before they vanished in puffs of smoke. And as Lyra's music played on, the Uriokh smuggler ship began to ignite. In fact, fires sprang up all around the ship, and the Obsidianders began to cry out in alarm, as their ship became awash in flame.

Fiss'Q watched the growing conflagration with wounded amazement, for not simply the wood was burning, but the men, themselves, the sails. The magical fire simply bloomed throughout the vessel, and everyone aboard her. The men ran about screaming, their clothes and armor aflame, and they prayed to their Obsidiander gods for aid, while their ship floated out into the harbor, brightly burning to the waterline.

Lyra stopped playing, tears in her eyes, and put the instrument back into its case, while Arokhnai locals called out from their balconies in wonder at the spectacle of the burning ship, the screams of the doomed Obsidianders echoing out across the water.

Lyra looked at Fiss'Q and nodded.

"Now, we can go," Lyra said.

❖ ❖ ❖

Eight

Slindahl was not happy to see Fiss'Q. Her oldest sister, a courtesan-concubine of the Arokhnai merchant-prince Festavio A'laric, she had done very well for herself over the years. Festavio was a spice merchant of Arokhnai, and had made a fortune selling jungle-drawn spices to the Northlanders and others.

Fiss'Q and Lyra had appeared in the atrium of the Villa A'laric by way of the Shadowlands, raising an alarm among the house guards, who had awakened their mistress. Slindahl confronted Fiss'Q from the second-floor balcony, gazing down at them.

Slindahl was middle-aged, and still lovely in the way all Arokhnai women were lovely—which was to say that they had faces made for frescoes: strong-featured, big-eyed, sharp noses and broad mouths, with clear and unambiguous jawlines. Slindahl retained the favor of Festavio with her boundless wiles and copious curves.

"What are you doing here, Fiss'Q?" Slindahl asked. "You nearly scared the life out of my men."

"I need to shelter here, Slindahl," Fiss'Q said. "I'm sorry to call upon you at this unfortunate hour."

"Unfortunate," Slindahl said. "You're lucky Festavio's abroad. He'd be furious at the intrusion."

Fiss'Q knew Festavio well enough to know he would welcome her, and that is was Slindahl alone who was furious at the intrusion. The man loved having an association with the Shadow Senate by way of Fiss'Q. As the patron and protector of the Emerald District—the mercantile and artisanal district of Arokhnai—Fiss'Q was immensely popular with the merchants, who saw her as their patron and protectress.

"And my Belavarria tells me that there's a ship burning in the harbor, no doubt *your* doing," Slindahl said, referring to Slindahl's eldest daughter and Fiss'Q's niece, the ebullient Belavarria, who appeared by Slindahl's side as if conjured there. She was the sweetly youthful mirror of her mother, with the high cheekbones and large, dark, not-yet-hard eyes.

"What did you do, Auntie?" Belavarria asked.

"She didn't do it," Lyra said. "I did."

Slindahl and Belavarria looked down at the Black Bard without comprehension and with an air of umbrage, at least from Slindahl.

"The Senator's been wounded," Lyra said. "She needs your help."

Fiss'Q took a knee, composing herself. She *was* wounded, but was not eager to appear weakened in front of Slindahl.

"Wounded?" Slindahl asked, as she and Belavarria ran downstairs, while the house guards looked on. "You can't be wounded, Fiss'Q."

"And yet, I am," Fiss'Q said. "I can be wounded, and I have been."

Slindahl was never one to particularly understand Shadowlandish ways. She'd known that her sister had become one and had risen high in the political ranks of Arokhnai, but beyond that, there was not much appreciation for it. Slindahl was firmly rooted in the here and now, the acquisitive dictates of the tangible, the knowable, the attainable.

In the atrium, a fountain of the Stormqueen burbled, the goddess grinning and glaring at them, as water poured from the ewer she held aloft. Around them, sweet-scented sarconia bushes bloomed, their pinkish blossoms swaying in the evening breezes. Slindahl had Belavarria fetch a lantern, and they stood by Fiss'Q, who was doing her best to hold her composure, while still bleeding. The Shadowmancer's arrows had grievously wounded her. It had been a long time since she'd been so badly wounded. Shadowlanders had left the boundaries of mortality far behind them, so the sensation was unfamiliar to her. She did not know if she could die from the wounds received, but she certainly felt like death.

"What are we to do, then? Who did this to you?" Slindahl asked.

"Obsidianders. It's too complicated to explain," Fiss'Q said. "But I have come under attack, and need to shelter here."

Slindahl snapped a finger at one of the houseguards, a young man in Alaric house livery—a saffron sun against a yellow field.

"Double the watch," Slindahl said. Belavarria looked down at Fiss'Q with concern on her face.

"Are you going to die, Auntie?" Belavarria asked.

"Not just yet," Fiss'Q said. "Please, just let me rest here awhile. I won't be any trouble."

"You're *always* trouble, Fiss'Q," Slindahl said. "Trouble for me, trouble for my dear Festavio. Trouble for Belavarria, and all of my children. You are nothing but trouble, little sister. And you always were."

Fiss'Q grinned ruefully. Slindahl had always done what was expected of her, whereas Fiss'Q had forever bucked the expectations of others. Slindahl had given Festavio five children: Belavarria, the eldest daughter; Mercatio, the eldest son; Solangio, another son; Partinia, the younger daughter; and Par'lan, the youngest son.

As was common in Arokhnai, most of the children had taken up their family's business—Mercatio and Solangio typically sailed with their father, while Belavarria, Partinia, and Par'lan managed the spice trade and family finances in the city. None of them had—thankfully, as Fiss'Q saw it—yet become courtesans.

"You're just lucky that the others are with Shar'na," Slindahl said, referring to their other sister, another prominent courtesan-concubine, based in the Diamond District and bound to Carnanthas, the deft-handed jeweler.

"I know of Carnanthas," Lyra said, piping up. "Magnificent artisan."

"Yes, yes," Slindahl said. "Very beautiful. Such hands he has. And who are you?"

Lyra seemed only too happy to have been asked.

"I'm Lyra Longbow," she said. "The Black Bard."

Belavarria brightened at the mention of her.

"She's a musician, Mother," Belavarria said. "She's played for kings."

Slindahl's always appraising gaze washed over Lyra, who seemed to relish the attention.

"Northland kings?" Slindahl asked. "Hah. Barbarians, the lot of them. Hardly worthy of the name. Aren't they all Manticore vassals, now?"

"Northlanders are a challenging audience, I'll grant you that," Lyra said, taking out the Night's Violin from its case. "But I've had far more trying audiences of late."

"You're a Northlander, too, by the look of you," Slindahl said.

"I am," Lyra said. "Hightower-born."

"Hightower," Slindahl said. "The City of Swords. Where honor itself is weighed and measured by the moneylender's scale."

"Fine one you are to talk of honor, Slindahl," Fiss'Q said, coming to Lyra's defense against her sister's caustic tongue. Lyra was merely amused.

"She's not wrong," Lyra said, producing the Violin. "Hightower *is* a city of mercenaries."

At the sight of the wondrous instrument, both Slindahl's and Belavarria's big eyes went wider, still, while Fiss'Q sought to get to her feet. The last thing she needed was Lyra drawing more attention to them.

"It's beautiful," Belavarria said. "Absolutely lovely."

Lyra smiled at them and began to play a song. It was a soft tune, rendered softer still by the purring of the silver strings, and Fiss'Q could feel, as before, the potent magic of the instrument in the young woman's hands. The music seemed to enfold Fiss'Q in a pleasurable warmth, and, to her amazement, Fiss'Q could feel—and see—her wounds healing. The magic of the Night's Violin caressed her with its music, and, in moments, Fiss'Q felt not only better, but healthy and whole again, as if she had not danced before the Door of Death that night. Even her garments mended, until both they, and she, were whole again.

Slindahl and Belavarria were themselves captivated by the music, which swam in the atrium, enveloping all who heard it. All who did were, in their way, healed by the sonorous sounds of the instrument. Its touch upon them was unmistakable, and breath-taking.

"That is certainly useful," Fiss'Q said. She had been witness to what the Night's Violin could do, and understood why others might desire it. Fiss'Q also knew, in that moment, that her own destiny was bound up in this strange instrument. That she could not let this thing be taken from Lyra again.

"Miraculous! Are you recovered, Auntie?" Belavarria asked. Fiss'Q could, through her own Shadowsight, see the excitement and joy in her niece at this unexpected adventure delivered to her doorstep.

"I do feel much better, Bela," Fiss'Q said, eyeing Lyra, who smiled at her and slipped the instrument back into its case. "What song did you play, Lyra?"

"I played 'Stolen Arts and Wounded Hearts'" Lyra said. "It's a Sylvanni tune."

"It seems to have worked its magic on me," Fiss'Q said. "Incredible."

"What *is* that thing?" Slindahl asked. "I've never seen the likes of it."

"It's just my instrument," Lyra said. "As your daughter said, I'm a musician. More than that, in truth."

She snapped her hand out to Slindahl, who shook it uncertainly. Lyra shook Belavarria's hand, too. Fiss'Q was amused, as her niece seemed positively smitten.

"Since you're recovered, Fiss'Q, you'll be leaving, then?" Slindahl asked. "Lest you bring trouble down around us here?"

"No," Fiss'Q said. "Let us rest in one of your guest rooms, Slindahl," Fiss'Q said. "Lyra and I have to discuss things. We can be gone at dawn."

"See to it that you are," Slindahl said. "Go on, Bela. Fetch your jaw from the floor and show your Auntie and her special friend to some of our guest rooms."

Nine

Darha had watched the Obsidiander ship burn in the harbor with a measure of bemusement and fascination, as she daubed the blood that ran from her nose with a kerchief. The fool Barvikh had failed to stop the Shadowlander, and the musician had recovered her instrument again, despite their efforts.

It had been a wondrous spectacle, however. The bard's music had conjured up the fire, and the ship had burned, the men had burned. Everything had gone up in a spectacular blaze. Before the fire had broken out, Darha had wanted to flee to the ship, but, as she felt blood drip from her nose, even at a distance, she knew that she dared not risk it. As a sorceress, sensitive to such thing, the raw exercise of magic of this potency could make her bleed. Had she been closer, the may have bled rivulets. The magic of the instrument was undeniably great and terrifying. No wonder they wanted it. A weapon like this could change the Northwar forever.

No, Barvikh and the others had deserved their fate. The contract resided with her, and her alone, now, to do with as she willed. The Shadowmancer was not uncomfortable with this, in truth. She was used to working alone, and was well-suited for it.

She'd taken stock of her performance against Fiss'Q, and decided she'd done rather well. Without the advantage of surprise, however, it would be a more difficult undertaking to proceed further. As a Senator of Arokhnai, Fiss'Q had power and privileges, connections that she might put to use to try to hunt Darha down.

While she was confident that she could deal with a Shadowlander one-to-one, there were so many of them in Arokhnai, and her chances against them were nonexistent. This required a reappraisal on her part, and a change in tactics and strategy.

The locals watched the ship burn to her waterline, the smoke and flames vanishing as the water rushed in and drowned them. Charred bodies of Obsidianders floated in the harbor, as well as debris. No one but Darha would know how it happened.

But the awareness of it weighed heavily upon her. She hadn't expected Fiss'Q to give up the fight with her. She'd expected her to carry it through, which would have bought Barvikh and the others enough time. That she'd run away before Darha had been able to talk to her was perhaps understandable, but threw everything off. She'd wanted to incapacitate the Senator so that they could parley. From what she'd heard about Fiss'Q, the woman almost never abandoned a fight. She'd been banking on that, only to have her flee.

Watching the ship's fire snuff out, bathing the Emerald District in darkness once again, except for the efforts of the Lamplighters and the arrival of the black-helmed City Watch, everything went back to normal. Fires happened in cities all the time. Darha knew they would console themselves that nothing unusual had occurred, as ordi-

nary people so often did. To the unwary eye, it just looked like a curious and unfortunate accident.

However, as she swabbed her nose again with her kerchief, Darha had no ignorance of what had transpired to cocoon her. Rather, she had a larger problem to solve.

Darha flexed her fingers, gazed at the runes on her fingernails, which she'd so carefully drawn in anticipation of the contract. She could see that one of her fingernails—the pinky finger of her left hand, had lost its iridescent rune, and was a normal fingernail again, as it had been before she'd undertaken her ritual.

"Nine lives left," Darha said, smiling to herself. The Shadow Prince would have His due eventually. He did not take kindly to the machinations of the Shadowmancers, it was said. She wondered when He had come for her—had it been during the fight? Had the ward been broken when Fiss'Q had attacked her? Or perhaps when she'd spirited the Violin away? She had not known. It was not wise to cross paths or swords with the gods. Everyone understood this, but Darha was not to be deterred.

Had she been other than who she was, she might have avoided taking on the risks inherent in Shadowmancy. Had she been prudent, she would not have followed that path at all. There were many safer, more lucrative routes in Ansible for aspirants.

But the shadows themselves had spoken to Darha, and she'd known it was her destiny. As night fully bloomed in Arokhnai, Darha retreated back into the darkness, with a mind to how she would yet salvage the day.

That meant finding Fiss'Q and negotiating with her.

Ten

The guest rooms at the Villa A'laric was sumptuous, but Fiss'Q expected no less of her sister, who was a creature of creature comforts. Slindahl was always a sensualist, and while Fiss'Q had only ever been in the villa as a young woman, it pleased her to see her sister doing well, by way of the careful arrangements made by their parents, and her lover-patron's successful business pursuits.

Fiss'Q worried that the Shadowmancer might return to attack An'Alta and her other servants, but there was little she could do about it at the moment, and she had taught An'Alta well enough that the young lady would be able to give as good as she got, if it came to that.

In the room, the walls were painted an agreeable goldenrod color that took up the lantern light and played as nicely with the polished hearthwood wardrobes and hand-carved, wood-framed bed. A lovely painting of the harbor hung on one of the walls, and Belavarria hovered nearby, pleased that Fiss'Q had seen it.

"I painted that, Auntie," Belavarria said.

"It's lovely, Bela," Fiss'Q said. "You have a good eye and a steady hand."

Her praise pleased her niece, who smiled and blushed, while Lyra looked on, smiling to herself as she set the instrument case on an amberwood chair in a corner of the room.

"My mother is afraid I'm going to look to you for mentorship," Belavarria said. "The way you did with Lord Q'rr'k when you were my age. We're all very proud of what you've done for the family. Even my mother, although she'd never show it. You've always been there for us, Auntie."

Fiss'Q had, indeed, been there for all of her siblings, after she'd become a Shadowlander. It had been Fiss'Q's own validation of her decision. As a woman of influence in one of the richest cities on Irth, it was the least she could do for her family. Her parents had not been happy about it, but there was nothing they could do about that.

"I don't think your mother would at all approve of me mentoring you," Fiss'Q said.

"No, she wouldn't," Belavarria said. "She says you're half-demon, now."

"Only half?" Fiss'Q said, smirking. "I shall have to try harder, clearly."

Fiss'Q smiled to herself. Slindahl wasn't far off. Belavarria glanced over her shoulder, as if fearing her mother would be there.

"I want to become like you, Auntie," she said. Fiss'Q reached out and hugged her niece a moment. The warmth and love she bore for her was as restorative as the magic of the Violin. Maybe even more so.

"You don't want this, Bela," Fiss'Q said. "I would never want to take the risk with you."

The drinking of the darkness that created a Shadowlander was always a perilous, capricious undertaking, and

Fiss'Q could not imagine risking Bela's life and sanity on the hopes that she would come through unscathed.

"But I want it," Belavarria said. "I fear that Mother's grooming me to become a courtesan like she was. I don't want that life. You didn't take that life, Auntie."

"My path is a more dangerous one, Bela," Fiss'Q. "You are sweet and sensitive, and truly talented in your art. I fear what the darkness might do to you. I'd rather encourage you to develop yourself as an artist. It's a more fitting pursuit for someone with your talent."

Fiss'Q keenly felt Belavarria's consternation. Her own trek toward the shadows had been a conscious act of rebellion, a refutation of the plans her parents had made for her. Lyra looked on, clearly fascinated by this exchange.

"Your aunt is trying to protect you," Lyra said, but Belavarria was undaunted. Fiss'Q smiled, for she could see much of her sister's stubbornness in the girl, and something of Fiss'Q's own determination to find her own way, amidst all of that youthful innocence.

"To become a Shadowlander is to turn your back on the life you led," Fiss'Q said. "And to become enmeshed in a trackless, roiling sea of shadowy complications, Bela. You need to taste more of the mundane world before you drink the darkness. You're too young."

"I'm practically a woman," Belavarria said, folding her arms.

She wasn't wrong, and Fiss'Q knew that there were other Shadowlanders in Arokhnai who might have eagerly taken on Belavarria as a protégé. To her knowledge, there were no Shadowlander dynasties—the toll inflicted by the Prince of Shadows was too steep for families to risk one another, the outcome too uncertain.

63

"Come back to me when you've become a woman, Bela," Fiss'Q said. "And I shall mentor you as I am best able. Just understand that your mother will be furious with me for doing so, and furious with you, if you seek the Path of Shadow."

Belavarria brightened at the prospect, and Fiss'Q felt sympathy for her niece. So young and bright and full of hope, willing, even desperate to change her stars. Fiss'Q understood that need. Fate was only fate if you resigned yourself to it.

"Thank you, Auntie," Belavarria said, hugging Fiss'Q fiercely. "It's all that I ask."

Her niece then left Lyra and Fiss'Q alone, glancing back at them with something close to stars in her eyes.

"Sweet child," Lyra said. "You wouldn't actually make her a Shadowlander, would you?"

"I absolutely would not," Fiss'Q said. "The Shadow Prince would love to have her."

Lyra looked confused.

"But you just tried to deter her," Lyra said.

"Of course I did," Fiss'Q said. "That's the only responsible thing to do. However, if she seeks me out when she's become a woman, why *wouldn't* I mentor my own niece? Slindahl will want to kill me, but not everyone's fated to become a courtesan. And Slindahl's own motivations in this are far less than pure. Just as my parents were. I became a pariah in my own family for what I did, but they all depend on me, now. If I were to truly rebuff Bela, she'd find another, less discerning mentor among my peers. I can't have that."

"So, you stall her while holding out a promise you have no intention of keeping," Lyra said.

"More or less," Fiss'Q said. "She's a skilled painter. I'll make the necessary arrangements to get her apprenticed to one of Arokhnai's more skilled painters. Give her enough of a taste of the here and now and she'll hopefully forget the allure of the Shadows."

"What a contradictory creature you are, Senator," Lyra said. She smiled, resting her hand on Fiss'Q's forearm. "I know how your family feels. My life is in your hands, now, Senator."

"Please," Fiss'Q said. "You don't need to call me that."

"But I like to," Lyra said. "It's so stately. It's a measure of respect."

Fiss'Q took up Lyra's offered hand and kissed the back of it, and then the palm. Her musician's hands were limber and strong, yet sensitive.

"You healed me," Fiss'Q said. "You saved *my* life, Lyra."

"The Violin healed you," Lyra said. "I cannot heal."

"You played the tune," Fiss'Q said. "You healed me with your heart."

Then she pulled Lyra to her and kissed her. The bard tasted sweet, like cloves. Lyra kissed her back harder still, and the two embraced, their bodies against one another as they stood in the room.

"You threw yourself headlong into danger on my behalf," Lyra said. "With neither care nor hesitation."

"It's in my nature," Fiss'Q said, guiding Lyra to the bed, though she hardly needed guidance. Lyra's limber hands slipped Fiss'Q free of her clothes, while Fiss'Q worked quickly on Lyra, until the two of them were against each other, skin-to-skin—Lyra's pale, Northland flesh against Fiss'Q's own inky skin, Lyra's warmth against Fiss'Q's coolness, her grey eyes gazing into Fiss'Q's red.

Although Fiss'Q pursued her own amorous efforts with the rigor she applied to all aspects of her life, she could not say in that moment whether she was seducing Lyra, or whether Lyra was seducing her.

It was a communion, as much as it was a melody attained between them. If Fiss'Q, by her nature as a Shadowlander, was no longer entirely alive, in Lyra's warm and ardent arms, she knew beyond a shadow of a doubt that night that she was far, far from dead.

Eleven

Darha had sheltered with the luthier in the Emerald District, taking care to wear some soft black gloves to cover her hands, and a cloak to cover her face and silver eyes. She did not want to draw attention to herself, lest the City Watch or another Shadowlander discover her.

The luthier's shop was small, but the upstairs had a little balcony that overlooked the city street. Only in Arokhnai would even a luthier take such steps to have such an enchanting residence.

However, Kaden had not been happy to see her return, but he dared not stand against her, so he let her in with a scowl on his old face.

"You were *supposed* to secure the instrument, Shadowmancer," Kaden said. "After I had done all the legwork for you."

"*You* were supposed to keep her at your shop when I arrived with the Obsidianders," Darha said. "What happened?"

"She's not one to be detained," Kaden said. "I'm an old man, not some goon. I gave you word as soon as she'd showed up. It's not my fault that she wanted to see the Senator, or that your Obsidianders were slow to answer the call."

Darha could not blame the man, but she did, all the same.

"Can you make a credible copy of the instrument from what you saw?" Darha asked.

"Of course I can," Kaden said. "But what's the point, now? From what I've heard, everyone's talking about the burning of the ship in the harbor. That was Abbasa's boat, yes? And your way out?"

"Yes, it was Barvikh's," Darha said. "He's dead, along with all the rest. The Black Bard killed them with a song from the Violin."

Kaden's old eyes widened at the thought of it.

"Truly?"

"What did I just say?"

"Such a sight it must have been," Kaden said.

"Yes," Darha said. "Wondrous. How long would it take you to make a copy?"

"A couple of weeks to build it, and a couple of months to varnish it," Kaden said.

"Hmm," Darha said. "Lord Abbasa's war fleet is already sailing for Arokhnai. They'll be here in days."

"What's the point, anyway?" Kaden asked. "With Barvikh dead, Abbasa's not going to want to see you."

He wasn't wrong.

"Build the instrument, anyway," Darha said. "On my commission."

Kaden's eyes narrowed, as anyone from Arokhnai's would when faced with the possibility of profit.

"It won't be cheap," Kaden said. "It's a beautiful instrument."

"I'm prepared to pay," Darha said.

"To what end?" Kaden asked. "The Black Bard parades around with the thing. She all but flaunts it."

"Let me worry about that," Darha said. "What I want is a credible counterfeit, one that would pass all but the most discerning of inspections. The fact of it is that even people who've heard of it have never seen it. And, for most, all they're going to see is a glossy black violin. So, make that, and we should be fine."

"It will cost you," Kaden said.

"Just make sure it doesn't cost me too dearly, or you'll be the one who ends up paying for it, Kaden," Darha said. "Now, get to it, and don't bother me. I'm going upstairs to rest."

Kaden glowered at her, but Darha ignored him and went upstairs.

"It's not a lodging house," Kaden called after her. "It's *my* home."

Darha cursed that she was born in Ansible, and not Arokhnai. She was not yet comfortable in this place, even though she'd been in Arokhnai for weeks in anticipation of the Obsidiander attack. When she had tracked the Black Bard to Arokhnai, she had made the necessary preparations.

As Darha faced the morning, she watched the merchants and tradesfolk ply their way on the peaceful and happy city streets from the balcony, while she brewed herself some blackleaf tea. How different it was in this place, versus her hometown.

In Ansible, the Wizards Militant ruled, and the city was dominated by caravans of magi, self-importantly parading about, flaunting their power. Ansible did not so much live in the shadow of the magi, as it was enslaved to them. Every waking moment of the city was bound up in the whims of wizards.

Here, in Arokhnai, people did not walk in fear. Darha could see this from her view on the balcony. The air smelled of sea breezes and fruit trees. People were free, here. Even the duplicitous Kaden was happy in his work. There was solace in that.

When she had negotiated the contract, Darha had imagined the feared Shadowlords of Arokhnai as far darker versions of the wizards of Ansible—self-important, domineering, commandeering—palanquins promenading through the city, on wizardly business. Darha had grown up on Ansible's streets, having proven herself intelligent enough to be able to apprentice to a wizard, a gimlet-eyed alchemist named Gliff.

Gliff had been obsessed with the Shadowlanders. He'd made them his life's work, trying to divine their dark secrets. Darha had proven to be the best of his apprentices, had devoted considerable time tending to his bottles and beakers with care and attention that exceeded the ability and inclination of the others. He'd kicked the others out, made her his assistant. They hated her for it, but Darha hardly cared—she was in, they were out, and, in Ansible, that was all that mattered.

Gliff had a close-cut black beard and hair, although he was old. It was one of his most meager yet marketable of creations, the dye that he used to make himself appear not as wizened as he was. It was also one of his most lucrative, and he sold a lot of it. And Darha, as his assistant, had spent much time making it.

"Shadowlanders are made, not born," Gliff said, pouring some ground-up sapphire dust into a concoction he'd been

commissioned to create by the Wizards Militant. "I don't know *how* they are made, but know that they *are* made."

"You think it's some sort of elixir, Master?" Darha asked, as she was stirring, stirring, stirring the hair dye. There were dozens of bottles of it to be poured, and Gliff would flog her if she spilled a drop. He sold every bottle at a hefty price.

"I *know* it is," Gliff said. "I just can't get at the nature of it. Shadow, of course. Obviously. A dullard slave could make that determination. But how to drink a shadow? That's the question. Let alone bottling it. No one has ever solved it. And we've tried. Who wouldn't want to become a Shadowlander—they live forever, you know? Did you know that? Another alchemical dream—immortality. Every wizard strives for it, whether here in Ansible or those Northland fools in Valdikan. And those jackanapes in Arokhnai have discovered it."

Darha's forearms ached and burned from all the stirring, but Gliff's formula required it, and he would accept nothing less than perfection for his clients. As Darha gazed into the great vat of black dye, she thought of the Shadowlanders.

"I could find it for you, Master," Darha said, making Gliff laugh. His laugh was not a pleasant sound, but was, rather, an acidic, creaking thing, filled to the brim with mockery and malice borne of hard experience.

"You? You, Apprentice?" Gliff asked. "The finest wizards in Ansible have sought to divine the secret for seventeen centuries, without success, and you think *you* can uncover it? Ah, the fresh-faced and matchless temerity of youth. Keep stirring."

But Darha had researched it in what little free time Gliff left her, and, if she had not uncovered the secret of the Shadowlords of Arokhnai, she had uncovered Shadowmancy. It had been a gift. Gliff had been less than impressed.

"Shadowmancy?" Gliff asked on another tiring day in his laboratory. "Are you mad?"

He had her busy with a mortar and pestle, grinding up components for yet another of his concoctions. In this case, she was grinding up seashells for what would be turned into an anti-aging salve. He'd gotten baskets of the shells brought in, of a particular type, and Darha had been put to work sorting through them and finding the specific type Gliff preferred, and placing them into other baskets. Having done that, he'd instructed her to grind them up to a fine powder. It was exhaustingly slow work, made more so by Gliff's relentless hovering over her.

"Shadowmancers are worse than demonologists," Gliff said. "Worse than fire wizards or necromancers, even. Their work consumes them. Mark my words: alchemy alone is the true future of magic. Practical, necessary, always in demand. Don't go chasing shadows, Apprentice. Keep grinding."

But while she did keep grinding, Darha could not banish the thought of Shadowmancy, once it had formed in her head. There were no known living practitioners of it. No magic was forbidden in Ansible, but there were no living Shadowmancers. Where had they gone?

In fact, the city depended on a vigorous trade in magic to survive. Whether genuine or charlatan magic, Ansible thrived in the perception of it as a magical city. Only distant Valdikan, with its libraries and colleges of magi, even came close to Ansible in its attention to magic and reputa-

tion. But where the magi of Valdikan were more scholarly in their approach to magic, Ansible was where far more practical pursuits of magic were explored. Ansible was the city for the working wizard.

Darha's biggest challenge was uncovering works of Shadowmancers, because whenever she'd bring it up, the archivist or clerk would simply scoff. Shadowmancy was nearly a forbidden art, even by the accommodatingly flexible ethical standards of Ansible.

"Why do people fear the Prince of Shadows?" Darha asked, when she'd returned from picking toadstools from a list that Gliff had prepared for her. She'd fetched two baskets of them from the graveyards of Ansible, including Lady's Grace, Hezeka's Kiss, and Velvet Strangler. Gliff was clearly making a batch of potent poison for a client of consequence in Ansible.

Hearing the name of the Prince of Shadows, Gliff genuflected to unseen gods with warding gestures.

"Don't bloody say His name, Apprentice," Gliff said. "You think I want Him looking in on me?"

"What have we to fear from gods, Master?" Darha asked. "We're Ansibleans. We fear nothing. *I'm* not scared of my own shadow."

"You should be," Gliff said. "Shadows follow us everywhere. *They're* everywhere we are. Nothing and no one is closer to you than your shadow. The Shadowlands are all around us, unseen. It's a mirror of this world, layered atop it, with the shadows as the gateways. Some say the Shadow Prince was envious of the world of Man, and in His mad envy, He'd copied the world in His own dark image. Of all the gods of Irth, He alone has persisted in this way—always there, but seldom seen. The others, they went off to godly places, far away from mortal eyes. But the Shadow Prince, He lingered. He watches. The Shadowlanders courted Him long ago, and He welcomed them into His arms. They are His chosen people."

Darha separated out the mushrooms into their own separate baskets, as Gliff was preparing three special cauldrons to brew a particularly deadly trio of poisons from them. With poison work, he took extra care, donning a mask and gloves. For Darha, tasked only with the harvesting and separation of the mushrooms, there was no protection.

"What of the Shadowmancers, then?" Darha asked.

"Interlopers," Gliff said. "Intruders in the Land of Shadow. Unwelcome and unwanted."

Darha had devoured the scrolls and texts she'd managed to find on Shadowmancy. Even the names of the Shadowmancers appealed to her—Lorthas the Strange. Black Anjilla. Vortian Shadowchaser. Karna Bloodthorn. They had danced with the shadows in antiquity and had made names for themselves, both in life and in their spectacular ends.

Lorthas the Strange had been strangled to death by his own shadow in broad daylight on the streets of Ansible, before a crowd of terrified onloookers.

Black Anjilla had been assassinated by a group of Shadowlanders who had ambushed the witch on her weekly trek into town, in the market square, in a bloody battle that was still remembered, although it had happened three centuries ago, as the Dance of Shadows.

Vortian Shadowchaser had actually lost his own shadow somehow, and had gone raving mad, hanging himself

from the High Tower of Ansible. It was said that even in death, his shadow had not returned to him.

Karna Bloodthorn had, after learning her craft, traveled north to her coven of Northland noble witches, where it was said that she'd wedded a dragon, only to be devoured by her draconian spouse on their wedding night.

Most precious of the books Darha had acquired was *The Book of Long Shadows*. It was a beautiful grey book of skateskin, with the sigil of Sireas Longshadow on the front of it. Although not the most flamboyant of Shadowmancers, Sireas had been the most enthusiastic scholar of the art, and had carefully documented the practice of Shadowmancy on its pages. Longshadow's other noteworthy accomplishment was producing scores of these books. He had hired scribes to produce them, and had widely distributed them for a decade before the Shadowlanders came for him, cutting him down and dragging him off into the Shadowlands.

Darha had worked a trade with the book vendor, having stolen some of Gliff's potions—an aphrodisiac, a bottle of poison, and a potent hallucinogen—for which the vendor was only too happy to part with *The Book of Long Shadows*.

"It's bad luck," the vendor had said, eagerly clutching the potions to his chest. "That book be damned, like all Shadowmancy."

Darha had devoured *The Book of Long Shadows*, finding sanctuary in the careful instruction of Sireas. She had to take care to not draw attention to herself while she studied it, lest Gliff get angry at her for being distracted from her alchemy.

Sireas would have been a good mentor for her. He seemed careful and kind, not gruff, embittered, and de-

manding as Gliff was. Gliff was never satisfied with the work she did. There was always some new way that she had failed him.

While she worked for Gliff, she stole other bottles of his potions, ointments, and essential oils and traded them for more books on Shadowmancy—*The Quality of Shadow*, *The Art of Nonexistence*, *The Ephemeralia*.

As she worked her way through them, Darha was confident that no one living in Ansible, or maybe the world, itself, knew more than she did about Shadowmancy. Gliff had noticed, and he had not approved.

He confronted her about it on that fateful day, after she'd been studying Shadowmancy in secret for over a year.

"Stealing my potions to buy books, Apprentice?" Gliff asked, storming into her room. The old man was fuming. "You think I don't take inventory? Inventory and alchemy are the most intimate of bedfellows, you young fool!"

"I'm no alchemist," Darha said. "I'm a Shadowmancer."

Gliff's scorn actually overwhelmed his rage at her theft of his tonics.

"You're nothing of the sort," Gliff said. "I warned you not to chase shadows, Apprentice. Now, you'll pay."

He reached for a black leather pouch of powdered poison, what Darha knew to be Death's Kiss, a particularly potent poison that was harmless to the touch, but lethal if inhaled.

But Darha had been ready for this confrontation for some time, and called forth the shadows, and was pleased when they answered. She caused the ones around them to lengthen and grasp for Gliff, wrapping around his arms and legs, and, most importantly, his mouth.

Not that she had anything to fear from an alchemist. For all of the vaunted practitioners of magic in Ansible, alchemists were both the most useful and the least threatening.

"I've learned all that I can from you," Darha said. "Now, off you go."

Darha watched the shadows tear Gliff apart, miming her own hand gestures, and saw his remains vanish in the shadows, until it was like Gliff had never been. She banished the shadows she'd conjured forth and set about taking over Gliff's business. She'd killed him, but not a drop was spilled. As an alchemist's apprentice, she took professional pride in that.

Gliff had been in good standing with the Guild of Alchemists, and had paid his dues, so Darha had been able to sell off his inventory readily on the market. His reputation was such that his products could command a good price.

When people came around looking for Gliff—whether peers, rivals, competitors, or clients—Darha had managed them all, saying that Gliff had gone forth looking for rare botanicals in Mercanto, and was not expected back for months. In the meantime, Darha handled trades and negotiated deals on her own with the patrons who turned up.

Those months after her murder of Gliff were precious memories for Darha, a time when she was able to set her own pace, working through Gliff's copious inventory to pay her way, while delving deep into her shadow magic during the night.

It had changed her irrevocably. And, best of all, no one noticed, even as she bought every book and scroll she could find on Shadowmancy in Ansible. Ansible was such a busy city, no one paid attention to the shadows all around them.

This saved her life, as Darha had given herself her silver eyes through an incantation buried deep within *The Ephemeralia*, which gave her the Shadowsight—the ability to see in this world and in the Shadowlands.

This ability to see between the worlds had let Darha become aware of the plotting of the Guild of Alchemists, who had filed a complaint about Darha to the Wizards Militant over the disappearance of Gliff, and his apprentice conducting business in his absence. With enough warning, Darha had been able to steal away in the night, taking her books with her, as well as Gliff's own alchemical formulas, and set his laboratory on fire.

She had fled to a ship bound for Uriokh, and had left Ansible behind her.

Darha drank her tea and smiled to herself. Every Shadowmancer had met a nasty end. It was a risk of the profession. But the others were not her. Darha had the benefit of hindsight, could see what the others had—and hadn't—done. She'd taken precautions. Whether those precautions protected her or not remained to be seen.

Further, in that vein, there was the matter of the Obsidiander war fleet sailing for Arokhnai. It was Barvikh's father and brothers, who had been sailing for Arokhnai in anticipation of the successful recovery of the Night's Violin. They would have expected to rendezvous with *The Wind's Kiss*, the smuggling ship that had burned in the harbor. By her estimation, they would realize Barvikh was overdue in a day or so, which would put them three days away from Arokhnai, with favorable winds.

What Lord Abbasa would do depended very much on his mood. Darha found him, like all Obsidianders, terribly full of himself and very proud. He would be enraged that Barvikh was delayed, and might press on without the prize. Uriokh deeply resented Arokhnai's dominance of the sea trade, and the Obsidianders were intent on ending that.

The question for Darha was whether she would expend any effort—and energy—to reach Lord Abbasa and warn him, or whether she would leave the man to his fate. Lord Abbasa was a very "kill the messenger" sort of man. She had seen this personally. He would receive the news of his eldest son's death very poorly, and her own failure to recover the Night's Violin more poorly, still. It would be foolish for Darha to risk herself to warn the Obsidianders. Far better for her to simply hang back and let that play out, while Kaden built the counterfeit violin.

In the meantime, she had the more important matter at hand, in the recovery of the Night's Violin. If only she could play the instrument, what a world she could create. Far beyond anything anyone could imagine.

Twelve

Fiss'Q and Lyra slept well, much to the consternation of Slindahl, who banged on the door with her knuckles an hour past dawn.

"Get up, Fiss'Q," Slindahl said. "We're not a boarding house."

Although she hardly needed sleep, it was a pleasant distraction to do so in the arms of Lyra, who slept quietly. Fiss'Q got out of bed and slipped on her tunic, her leggings, bodice and boots, and strode over to the instrument case, which she opened.

The Night's Violin looked as lustrous as ever, its lacquered wood almost luminous, with the hint of runes along its edges, something she hadn't seen before. The silver strings beckoned, but Fiss'Q knew better than to pluck them. Disaster awaited anyone who hit a sour note on the instrument. It was part of its curse, and one that had led to stories Fiss'Q could recall mostly because of the grisly character of them.

Like Thumbless Jon of Windhaven, who had drunkenly attempted to pluck out a ditty on the instrument on a dare, earning his name as a half-mad, wandering vagrant ever since. There was also the mad minstrel of Mercanto, who had turned himself into a ghost by playing a tune with it. He was still said to haunt the streets of Mercanto, searching for his lost instrument. It was around that time that the war wizard Farro had taken the instrument and secured it in Valdikan.

"Such trouble you cause," Fiss'Q said to the instrument, which was as mute as ever.

"I was born to it," Lyra said, from over her shoulder. "Both my parents were mercenaries. Can you believe that? My mother with her breechbow, part of the Quarrelers. My father was a sword-for-hire. They're both dead, now, but they were at it a long time."

Fiss'Q knew of the Quarrelers. They were a company of women mercenaries in Hightower who specialized in their crossbows. That Lyra had become a musician was a curious departure from the livelihoods of her parents.

"This instrument is powerful, Lyra," Fiss'Q said. "You'll not be safe so long as you possess it."

Lyra appeared beside her, putting her arms around Fiss'Q, who was taller than she was, and leaner.

"Fallryn said the same thing. Who wants to be safe?" Lyra asked. "I wouldn't do what I do if I wanted to be safe. Or to play it safe."

She snatched up the Night's Violin and began to play a tune with it, something lilting and sprightly. In the close confines of the room, the music was beyond beautiful, and, as she played, Fiss'Q became aware of the scent of green-leaf tea and freshly baked orange and feyberry scones.

On the trunk table at one end of the room, Fiss'Q could see the two porcelain cups as well as a pot of tea, and the dishes upon which the scones sat, beside a ramekin of butter.

Lyra stopped playing, winking at her.

"You see?" Lyra asked. "I just made us breakfast. Nothing scary about that."

The cheeky show of power in this trivial fashion alarmed Fiss'Q more than she dared let on. She walked over and picked up a cup. Inlaid on it were musical notes, black against the white of the porcelain, as if captured from the air itself.

"You shouldn't play with it that way," Fiss'Q said, picking up the warm scone and buttering it. She tasted it, and it was delicious.

"Oh, don't scold me, Senator," Lyra said. "I was simply playing. I'm playful, after all. It's something we troubadours are, after all. We are nothing, if not playful."

Fiss'Q was not averse to playing, herself, but this was on another order of magnitude. It wasn't the same as juggling daggers, or leaping from rooftop to rooftop. The Night's Violin was not a toy or a trifle. It was old magic, and powerful magic. Fiss'Q could feel it with each note Lyra played.

The bard put away the instrument and fetched herself her tea and scones, while Fiss'Q found her mind wandering through the myriad possibilities of the instrument. They were staggering to imagine. Anyone who could play the Night's Violin could make whatever they wanted to happen a reality.

"You've made quite a problem for me, you know," Fiss'Q said. "You can't leave Arokhnai with it."

Lyra laughed, drinking her tea. Her laughter carried with it both mockery and insecurity, to Fiss'Q's well-tuned ear. As a Senator of Arokhnai, nuance was a second language to her.

"But I must wander, all the same," Lyra said. "It's in my nature to do so. I can't stay rooted in one place. I wilt and wither."

"That is certainly a problem," Fiss'Q said. "On your own, you cannot possibly protect yourself against those who would try to steal the instrument. They will forever chase you down."

Lyra seemed insulted by the suggestion, pouting as she dressed. Her pout wounded Fiss'Q anew, bringing her actual pain. She would do anything but hurt Lyra, if she possibly could.

"I'm more resourceful than you know," Lyra said. "I've dealt with danger before. It's not easy doing and being who I am, Senator, I assure you."

"All the same, you came to me," Fiss'Q said. "I wouldn't entrust your protection to anyone but myself."

Lyra finished dressing, smoothing out wrinkles here and there. She was a vision in black, from head to toe. She was beautiful beyond bearing, and Fiss'Q wanted to take her yet again.

"Then you'll have to decide to accompany me wherever I choose to go," Lyra said. "Hightower taught me that the only way is to make your own way in this world, Senator. Arokhnai is paradise, but it's only one place. The world is full of places. I must see them all."

Belavarria rapped on the door.

"Mother wants to know when you'll be gone, Auntie," she said. "Sorry to bother you again."

Fiss'Q went to the door and opened it, seeing her niece standing there, looking terribly embarrassed, all knotted hands and half-chewing her lip, averting her gaze.

"Tell your mother we'll be gone before she even misses us," Fiss'Q said, giving Belavarria a hug and a kiss on the top of her head. She loved Belavarria as she loved all of her nieces and nephews, passionately, and without reservation. They kept her rooted in the here and now, which was essential for a Shadowlander.

"Remember what we talked about, Auntie," Belavarria said.

"How could I possibly forget it?" Fiss'Q said.

Lyra appeared at the door, toting the Violin.

"She also asked that you use the back door," Belavarria said. "To avoid drawing attention, since you're in trouble and suchlike."

"Oh, I'll do better than that," Fiss'Q said, holding out her hand to Lyra, who took it with a searching look in her eye. How lovely she looked in the morning, her black hair tousled and her sweet face all but heart-shaped.

Fiss'Q then parted the Veil, to the bedazzlement of her niece, who was a radiant burst of love and longing, and the two of them slipped out of the villa unseen, passing through the now-phantom walls as if they were not there.

They traveled across Arokhnai, to Fiss'Q's home, where it appeared An'Alta had already made arrangements with the Deathmen, for the bodies of the warriors were no longer there. There appeared to be no sign of the Shadowmancer, but Fiss'Q took little solace in that, given that she could hide from her Shadowsight.

Fiss'Q returned to the here and now, startling the other servants, who had been taking care to clean up her dwelling.

"Mistress, you're alive," An'Alta said, giving Fiss'Q a hug and a sidelong glance at Lyra, who pried her hand from Fiss'Q's.

"I am, An'Alta," Fiss'Q said. "Did you think I could be so easily killed as that?"

"We heard stories about the burning boat," An'Alta said. "We were terribly worried."

Fiss'Q had a pile of problems to deal with, and had to sort them out in her head. There was the immediate concern of the Shadowmancer, who posed a clear threat to her and Lyra. There was the prospect of the involvement of the Obsidianders, and whatever that meant. And there was the issue of keeping the Night's Violin safe with her in Arokhnai, versus letting Lyra run off with it.

The last concern was the greatest for Fiss'Q, because there was simply no way of resolving it to Lyra's satisfaction. The young woman's use of the Night's Violin at Valdikan alone had the direst ramifications. The Manticore would send agents her way until either the instrument was recovered or destroyed. Either way, Lyra was a walking dead woman. Her fate was sealed the moment she strode the battlements of Valdikan. It made Fiss'Q want to seek out the Manticore and end him, for Lyra's sake. But even she would not risk that herself, if there was to be a hope of victory. As skilled as she was, she could not defeat the Manticore alone, however much she wanted to.

Fiss'Q had to make her understand this danger. She glanced at Lyra, who was looking right at her with those grey eyes of hers, a mute challenge.

"This is the safest place for you," Fiss'Q said.

"I'm *not* staying here," Lyra said. "The world is more my home more than sweet Arokhnai."

"Lyra," Fiss'Q said. "I don't think you quite realize what you've done."

An'Alta and the others spirited themselves out of the room. They knew Fiss'Q well enough to know the tone of her voice, and what storms it brought with it.

"They needed me," Lyra said. "And I helped them. I saved that city. Should I have done nothing and let the city fall?"

"Of course not," Fiss'Q said. "But in so doing, you drew his eye. The Manticore has plenty of enemies, and the one thing I can assure you is that he will hunt you to the ends of the Irth, my dear. It's what brought you to me. You came to me for aid, and I've freely given it, without question. The Shadowmancer, we can't be sure why she's here, except to know that she wants the instrument. Here, with me, you are safe. I will never let anything happen to you."

"That's just it," Lyra said. "I *want* things to happen to me. Experience is my nourishment, as much as food and drink. I'm not one of your trophies."

Lyra's hand flew out in the direction of one of Fiss'Q's well-adorned walls.

"No, you're not," Fiss'Q said. "But I cannot in good conscience let you leave Arokhnai, now that you've come here. It's impossible."

"I should have stayed with Lord Fallryn," Lyra said. "I should never have come to Arokhnai."

Fiss'Q knew the Sylvanni well enough to divine what had likely happened.

"He sent you off, didn't he?" Fiss'Q asked.

"Hardly. He was enraptured by me. He wanted to spirit me to Solaria as his paramour," Lyra said. "As surely as you want to hold me captive in Arokhnai."

"'Captive' is hardly the right word for it," Fiss'Q said. "You are hardly a prisoner."

"Oh, but I am," Lyra said. "I'm cursed, aren't I? Even if I left the Violin here—which I will *not* do—the Manticore will send agents after me."

Something occurred to Fiss'Q that hadn't occurred to her before. There was no way Lord Fallryn, having slipped Lyra from Valdikan as he did, would have simply let her go. No self-respecting Sylvanni would do such a thing, with such a prize. He'd have faced the same quandary that Fiss'Q herself faced. The Night's Violin was too great a prize, too powerful a thing to let loose capriciously. Perhaps it had been part of Farro's gambit, a way for him to have unburdened himself of the task of guarding and protecting it. That made sense to her.

"Fallryn didn't let you go. You ran off. What happened to Fallryn?" Fiss'Q asked. "How did you escape from the Sylvanni?"

Lyra met her eyes with her own, and told that story, as well.

✥ ✥ ✥

Thirteen

While Kaden worked on the replica violin, Darha hunted the streets of Arokhnai, marveling anew at the joyful enterprise of its citizens. There was only the boundless promise of opportunity and industry in this city. Arokhnai bustled by day, and the markets swelled with products from around the world. This was a city untouched by war or privation. It was a city almost serene in its confidence, and that struck Darha deeply.

It was as different from Uriokh as it was from Ansible. The Obsidianders' slave city was old and beautiful. The whitestone buildings were rife with lovely Sorian relics and ancient architecture, but one could never travel far without hearing the crack of the whip, the barked orders of the slavers, the jingle of chains. That city-state was given over to its enterprise with a fervor that bordered on mania.

Darha had gone to Uriokh out of necessity, having fled Ansible under the cloud of sorcerous scandal and fear of retribution on the part of the Wizards Militant. In utilitarian Uriokh, a freewoman of her singular ability stood out, and it paid to lend her services to those who could afford to pay. And the slavers of Uriokh could afford to pay.

What's more, their hostility toward Arokhnai was itself profitable. Lord Abbasa had raged about it in his fortress-villa. Like his son, only far more so, Lord Korg Abbasa was a brash, stocky, black-bearded man with a voice that could shake the timbers of a sailing ship. Barvikh had taken Darha to him to make his pitch, after the two of them had crossed paths when Darha had wrapped up business with another client.

They had been received in his grand hall, a lengthy whitestone room with a great, rectangular blackwood table dominating it. Seeing that much blackwood spent on the creation of that mammoth table alone more than communicated to Darha the wealth and hubris of the Abbasa dynasty. If that was not enough, the far wall was given over to a huge tapestry that bore the flag of Uriokh—a black triangle on a white field, surrounded by a circle of grey chains.

The father and son were attended by a coterie of beautiful slaves, who poured them bloodwine and hovered nearby, while Lord Abbasa walked to the balcony that adjoined his grand hall, which overlooked the bustling harbor of Uriokh, filled with war galleys and tall-masted slave ships.

"I've brought you a gift, Father," Barvikh said. "This rogue sorceress of Ansible, Darha Lonai."

"I know who she is," Abbasa said, then glared at Darha with intent to intimidate. The man built his entire life around intimidation. But Darha had danced with shadows. She was not one to be intimidated, and she met his gaze evenly. What was a mundane man to a woman who had stared long and hard into the Land of Shadow?

"Then you know I can help you, Lord Abbasa," Darha said.

From the balcony, Uriokh's activity might have resembled Arokhnai's, but the scent of blood and fear hung about it. Always fear, soaked deep into the stone.

"You think you're the first to come to me this way, witch?" Abbasa asked. The goblets they drank from were hammered silver. Darha thought it was deliberate, given the special relationship silver had to the Shadowlanders.

"I'm not a witch," Darha said. "I'm a sorceress. Very different things."

Darha knew of witches, who roamed the wilderness, peddling poultices and portents, hoping to avoid the noose or the bonfire. The best of them lived in caves or cottages, far from the reach of ruthless men. While she bore witches no malice, she was not part of their sisterhood.

"Any woman touched by magic is a witch," Abbasa said. "And any man, as well. We do not traffic in witchcraft in Uriokh. You're a long way from Ansible, child."

Darha would not be hindered by the man's belligerent tone. Nor would Barvikh, it appeared.

"Father, she's here to help us," Barvikh said. "She brings word of something wonderful."

"Yes, by all means, tell me," Abbasa said, with exaggerated, mocking grandiosity.

"You know of the miracle at Valdikan," Darha said, deciding that cutting to the point would be best with the preening Abbasa patriarch. "Last year?"

"Yes, who *hasn't* heard of it?" Abbasa said. "The violin that turned an army of the Manticore into a sea of roses? A ridiculous story. Makes me want to know what *really* happened. Wizards, most likely."

"It's in Arokhnai," Darha said. "I mean to recover it."
"How do you know?" Abbasa asked.

"I have tracked it there," Darha said. It was a not a lie. She had done so once she'd heard the stories of what had happened there, the awestruck gossip of tradesfolk. Darha didn't trade in gossip, but when the stories kept coming in, she'd investigated, herself, consorting with the shadows for answers, and they had provided her those answers.

"So, recover it," Abbasa said. "Bring it to me, and I'll pay you for the trinket."

The man was such a fool. How so great a fool could come to run a city as powerful as Uriokh was another mystery Darha planned to explore with her shadows.

"I'll use it to open Arokhnai's armored harbor to you," Darha said. "You can send your fleet of ships to her shores and conquer the city."

"Ha," Abbasa said, draining his cup and holding it out for one of his slaves to fill. "The city crawls with Shadow-landers, Witch."

"I will have dealt with them," Darha said. "They will not trouble you. And your fleet can sail in and lay claim to Arokhnai, as you've always wanted."

"How could *you* know what *I* want?" Abbasa asked. "Did your shadows tell you what I wanted?"

"Everyone in Uriokh would like to see Arokhnai fall, would they not?" Darha asked.

Lord Abbasa drank again from his cup, while the slaves lurked nearby, watching him with frightened eyes. They looked to be Northlanders, likely refugees from the Northwar, easy pickings for the Obsidianders.

"Yes, you're right about that, Witch," Abbasa said. "My whole life I've grown up in the shadow—yes, the shadow, I said it—of Arokhnai. I would love to see her humbled. I would love to see her people in chains, marched out of

there as slaves of Uriokh. I would love to feed the Shadowlanders, themselves bound fast in silver chains, to the volcanoes. The looks on their lovely faces as they were thrown in, one after another, to Mortis and Vertis. It would be a glorious thing. But how would this supposed magic violin make this possible?"

"The Night's Violin makes anything possible," Darha said. "That is its blessing and its curse. It's in the possession of the Black Bard, the very one who wielded it at Valdikan. She's on the run, gone to Arokhnai for protection from the Manticore, the Sylvanni, too. But if *we* were to get it, and Arokhnai were to fall, then no city could stand before Uriokh."

The greed of Lord Abbasa lit his eyes, and he cackled a moment. Slavelords were ruled by greed, Darha found, above and beyond any other restraining inclination.

"This is what *you* need, Barvikh," Abbasa said. "This young witch has ambition. I like that in a person. So, let me see if I understand—Barvikh spirits you to Arokhnai. You acquire the violin, and you use it to disable the Shadowlanders' defenses. Whereupon I sail a battle fleet to take Arokhnai's harbor, and then we seize the city?"

"More or less, yes, Lord Abbasa," Darha said.

"You seem rather confident of your chances," Abbasa said. "Do you think you're the first person to attack Arokhnai? She's weathered many storms over the centuries."

"I'm a Shadowmancer," Darha said. "I can give them something they would not expect. And, with the Night's Violin, they would be helpless before me."

"So, you're a musician as well as a witch?" Abbasa said. "One would think the ability to play is critical to the use of the instrument."

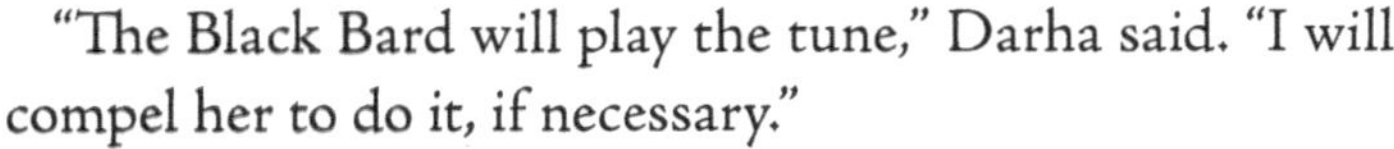

"The Black Bard will play the tune," Darha said. "I will compel her to do it, if necessary."

Abbasa laughed long and loud, and Darha looked quietly, while Barvikh watched.

"It's something they won't expect, Father," Barvikh said. "For too long, Arokhnai has ruled her stretch of sea uncontested. A war fleet from Uriokh would be just the thing to set them straight."

"How much time do you need, Witch?" Abbasa asked. "And how can you even be sure the instrument is in the city?"

"I *know* it's there," Darha said. "The shadows told me of its arrival. I've made contacts there, through my own means."

"Oh, the shadows told you," Abbasa said. "You'd have me deploy a war fleet because the *shadows* told you?"

Darha tossed aside the silver goblet, which clattered on the whitestone floor and wound her fingers into arcane knots, uttering words of power she'd studied so intently that they were etched deep into her mind, and called forth the shadows of Abbasa, Barvikh, and the slaves. They set upon the Obsidianders, grabbing them, holding them at bay.

"What is this?" Abbasa asked, straining against the grasp of shadows. "Witchcraft!"

"It's just a sample of what I can do, Lord Abbasa," Darha said. "I could kill the lot of you right now, if I wanted to. *My* shadows. Mock me if you like, but I'm offering you the bloody keys to Arokhnai."

Darha was sure the chill of the shadows was more than apparent to the slavelord, and she went to the balcony and leaned upon it, arms folded, while they struggled against the shadows. She raised a radiant finger and snapped it, and her incantation ceased, the shadows fled back to their natural places.

Lord Abbasa sputtered, his face pale with rage.

"The audacity of you, Witch," Abbasa said. "To lay hands on a Slavelord of Uriokh in this way?"

"Consider it a demonstration of my clear intent," Darha said. "I could have gone to the other slavelords, Lord Abbasa. I chose you, because you command the largest fleet. You're the most powerful. And the most ambitious, if I understand you well enough."

Abbasa had shaken off the cold and recovered himself, glaring at Darha. It was alright. She'd been glared at before.

"When I tell you that I have it on good authority that the Night's Violin is in Arokhnai, I ask only that you trust me," Darha said. "And that your fleet comes to pick me up when the time is right. A month hence, by the light of the full moon, when the shadows are long. Do that, and when the sun rises, Arokhnai will be yours, and yours alone."

"And what do you get out of this?" Abbasa asked. "What's in it for you?"

"I want all of the books of Arokhnai," Darha said. "Every scrap of parchment, every scroll, every tome. All mine."

"Books?" Abbasa asked, almost laughing, despite his anger. "You want books?"

"I'm an avid reader, Lord Abbasa," Darha said. "And the libraries of Arokhnai go back to ancient Soria. There is treasure there, for those who can decipher it."

Abbasa did laugh, then.

"Fine, Witch," he said. "You can have your books, if I can have Arokhnai."

Abbasa would not shake her hand, but the deal was struck, as sure as if it had been stamped in silver.

fourteen

"fallryn had taken me from Valdikan as he'd promised," Lyra said. Fiss'Q had taken them to the roof of her townhome, where a lovely garden grew—lemon trees, limes, oranges, bloodfruit, baneberry bushes—all of them carefully tended and groomed to create a pleasant and diverting sanctuary among the cedarwood planks.

The scent was heavenly, and the peace of the place was profound. "We traveled in the Sylvanni caravan, protected from attack by the Sylvanni and their reputation. They are a unique people. They watched me with the Violin with a measure of curiosity and contempt, something only the Sylvanni can manage, I assure you, Senator."

Fiss'Q nodded, sipping some of the Mercantish bluewine she'd had An'Alta bring up from the wine cellar. They drank from cut crystal cups, and Fiss'Q had lit a fire in the firepit, which burned pleasantly. An'Alta had brought up some spiced chops, which were sizzling over the open flame.

"'We should head north, to Solaria,' Fallryn said. 'I can protect you better there.' And I could see that he meant it. 'My Lord of Bluewater,' I replied. 'You know as well as I do that I could never live in Solaria, beautiful as it is.' Fallryn was not one to be dissuaded, however. 'You have done a wondrous thing, Lyra. But a dangerous thing, as well. Exceptions can, and will, be made on your behalf.' And, Senator, as I gazed into his beautiful eyes, his handsome countenance, I wanted nothing more than that. You know as well as I do how rare it is for a human to be offered passage into Solaria."

Fiss'Q knew, indeed. She had an old friend who had made that passage, in fact. Farys, the Wolf Knight, had grown up in Solaria as a boy. It was the rarest of gifts the Sylvanni granted, the pleasure of their company.

"I knew the stories of Solaria," Lyra said. "The forests, the mountains, the pure rivers. The eternal, unspoiled beauty of the place. The stories of men driven mad by the pristine perfection of it all. The harmony of it, that unique magic the Sylvanni bring to all that they touch. It was tempting. I can say without equivocation that I was tempted, Senator."

An'Alta emerged from the shadows to tend to the chops, taking them from the fire and plating them on beautiful blue and white plates, beside mashed and peppered beetroot and buttered hearthbread, still warm to the touch. Fiss'Q thanked An'Alta and took the plates, serving Lyra by her own hand. The Black Bard took the plate with thanks and set it beside her, continuing her story.

"We traveled south through the Leaguist Cities," Lyra said. "Already, the story of what had happened in Valdikan had traveled ahead of us, to Hightower, Windhaven, and Ravendale. We were received as heroes. The jubilation was wonderful to experience, and to be the source of it? I tell you, it was finer than anything. A symphony of hope, unlike anything I'd seen before. For too long, the

Manticore had conquered everyone he'd faced. He seemed unstoppable. And in my musical moment in Valdikan, that reckless moment, I had delivered a city from certain doom. Just me and the Night's Violin, making music that decided the day."

The bluewine and her memory of that moment made Lyra blush, and she paused to drink some more, while sampling some of the fire-seared chop and beetroot. She was so young, so full of hope. Fiss'Q enjoyed their intimate meal in her rooftop garden, beneath the stars. Up here, even the troubles of Arokhnai seemed far away.

"Fallryn was pleased by the attention, as well," Lyra said. "But as seeming part of my entourage—I know that's not what they were, but it felt that way, in that moment— the Sylvanni themselves basked in the glow of the people's adoration. People had been so hungry for hope, thanks to the Manticore's warmongering. It meant something to them. And if it meant viewing the Sylvanni with a less guarded gaze, it was well worth it. That's how I saw it. And we never overstayed our welcome—three weeks in each of those cities. Time enough to celebrate the victory, for the Sylvanni to conduct the trade they needed (and whatever other business they had intended), and for me to regale people with stories of my own adventures and garner my share of coin. It was wonderful. Coins fell to me like rain. Dinners, parties, entertainments, honors, and accolades. All for me."

Fiss'Q watched Lyra pause to take a few bites of food and a drink, wondering all the while what she should do with the Night's Violin. She could, of course, simply take the thing from Lyra. But she didn't want to do that. She

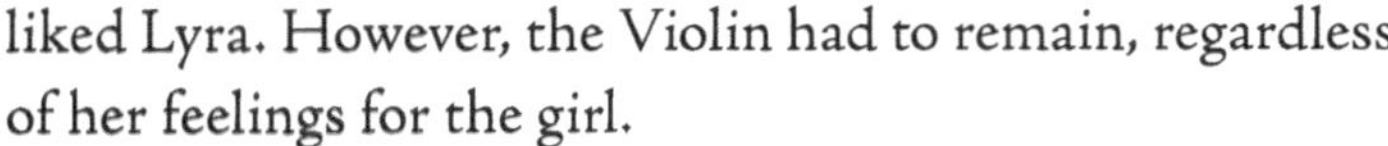

liked Lyra. However, the Violin had to remain, regardless of her feelings for the girl.

"What happened to Lord Fallryn?" Fiss'Q asked.

"We left Ravendale, and Lord Fallryn wanted to head north, toward Forj," Lyra said. "He said his people had lucrative trade arrangements with the Kingdoms of Hinterland and Westfall, and that the Dwarves of Forj would be happy to see them. And that I would be welcomed there, as well, for the citizens of Forj were no friends of the Manticore."

The Iron Knight protected, defended, and ruled the Leaguist City of faraway Forj, and Fiss'Q doubted that the Knight's minions would simply let the Sylvanni pass through their city-state without incident. To say nothing of the Dwarvish kingdoms. No, Fallryn was trying to steer Lyra north, toward distant Solaria. Whether he admitted it or not, that was his final destination.

"But you didn't go to Forj," Fiss'Q said.

"No," Lyra said. "Lord Fallryn and I had a difference of opinions. As much as I might have wanted to see the wonders of the mountain folk, I wanted to head south, to Old Soria. As wondrous as Forj no doubt is, I wanted to see Arokhnai, the Crown Jewel of the Southlands. Fallryn urged me not to take that path. 'The Shadowlanders rule Arokhnai,' he said. 'You will become their prisoner. Stay with me, that I may protect you from harm.' I could tell that he was sincere in his desire to protect me from harm, but I don't need anyone's protection. I've gotten through the world just fine on my own."

Lyra drank deep of her cup of wine, and Fiss'Q refilled it, knowing it would help keep the words flowing.

"Fallryn told me that their caravan had already been through Arokhnai earlier in the year, and that there was no reason for them to go back down there. 'Besides,' he said. 'We must head north through the mountains before winter closes the passes. Come with us, and I promise you will not be disappointed.' But my instincts were that if I went with him further on this journey, I would be a pampered prisoner of the Sylvanni. And, as much as I might desire to see beautiful Solaria, or even mythic and majestic Sylvannia, I would do so only at the loss of my freedom. So, with tears in my eyes, I played a mournful tune with the Violin and, like a ghost, disappeared before their beautiful eyes. Fallryn had set his bodyguards to try to stop me, but I had made myself insubstantial to their touch, as the music played. What's more, I dreamed of arriving at Arokhnai, at the very gates of the city, and, as I played and Fallryn beseeched me to remain with him, I vanished from their encampment and appeared at Arokhnai's doorstep, by the grace of the Violin. I tell you that I wept at the gates of Arokhnai, for my heart broke to leave gracious, handsome Fallryn that way. The look on his face when I passed out of his reach is something I will carry with me for the rest of my life. The sorrow of the Sylvanni is grief beyond imagining."

Fiss'Q smiled to herself. No doubt Fallryn was cursing himself for not prying the instrument out of the girl's hands before it had come to that. But, at least he had not come to harm, as Fiss'Q had feared. With the Night's Violin, anything was possible.

"You were right to come here," Fiss'Q said.

"Was I?" Lyra asked. "For now, Fallryn's comment holds true, for you do mean to make me a prisoner, as surely as he intended."

"A guest, not a prisoner," Fiss'Q said. "I would never imprison you, Lyra."

Lyra sulked into her cup, drank down the bluewine, which stained her teeth a bluish-white. Bluewine came from Sylvannia, and was painfully expensive. But it was delicious, as well, and that was enough for Fiss'Q.

"I'm only glad you came to us," Fiss'Q said. "And not one of the other cities of Soria. The wizard-lords of Ansible would have stolen your instrument as soon as they were able. Indeed, the sorceress who attacked us is from Ansible."

"I only want to perform," Lyra said. "I am no weapon of war. Nor is the Violin. We make such beautiful music, and this Manticore nonsense intrudes. Sometimes, I dream of appearing before the Manticore and striking a tune that would slay him. Can you imagine that? Me, the Black Bard, the slayer of the Manticore? I could end his war on the world with the stroke of my bow. And, the truth of it is that I would do so only so that I might travel the world in peace again, without fearing revenge from his acolytes."

Fiss'Q enjoyed the thought of that, but doubted the Manticore would be so easily caught unawares. He surrounded himself with courtiers, sorcerers, magi, witches, and demons. Lyra would have found herself captured and tortured, and would have delivered the Violin to him, which would have been the absolute worst of situations. A mind like the Manticore's would turn the Night's Violin onto the Irth and remake it in his monstrous image. Such a fate frightened Fiss'Q.

"Please promise me that you will never do that," Fiss'Q said. "At least not on your own. You would regret that decision the moment you made it."

"It's just a trifle," Lyra said. "A flight of fancy. I'm whimsical, Senator. I understand, however, that the Violin lets me do whatever I want. It empowers me. Whatever I play, whatever I think and feel in the song, it is made manifest."

"Yes," Fiss'Q said. "And that's why you must remain in Arokhnai. Or, at the very least, why the Violin must remain here."

The young woman's proud and lovely face soured at that prospect. She reached out for the instrument, in its case as ever, like an attendee at their meal. It was a protective, covetous gesture, childish in spirit.

"Wherever it goes, I go," Lyra said. "We are bound up inextricably, Senator. Now and forever."

In her youth, Fiss'Q would simply have taken the instrument from the girl by now. It would have been that easy. But she cared for Lyra, and would not treat her so impertinently. At least not yet.

"I understand that desire," Fiss'Q said. "But it's not practical, Lyra. The moment you accepted it from Farro, from the first note you played along the wall, you moved beyond the life you had before, and the life you must lead, now. Whatever you intended, what you did was undeniably heroic—it was brave beyond measure, especially given the Violin's history with those who've played it before."

"The moment was perfect for it," Lyra said. "To do something, I mean. I was simply moved by the moment, versus seeking to be a hero."

"As is the case with most acts of heroism, Lyra," Fiss'Q said. "No one ever can *plan* to be a hero; it simply is the

willingness on the part of the right person to do the right thing at the right time. And that makes all the difference. However, that's also my point—that moment has forever changed you. You cannot simply go back to the itinerant life you had before."

Lyra's youthful intransigence buttressed her against Fiss'Q's argument.

"I'm no puppet of the fates, Senator," Lyra said. "I make my own way."

"No longer," Fiss'Q said. "I respect your decisions, but as the keeper of that instrument, you have a responsibility to it, to yourself, and the world. The power of the thing, and your talent, they cannot be separated."

"Exactly so," Lyra said. "We cannot be separated."

Lyra set down her cup and reached for the instrument, opening it and pulling it forth from its case. In the firelight, the Night's Violin was as glossy as ever and even more beautiful.

She played "The Hymn for Lost Heroes", one that Fiss'Q knew as well as anyone, a mournful and beautiful ballad about a wandering knight seeking justice wherever it could be found, and, in the end, finding only death waiting for him, after a lifetime of duty.

While she played, Lyra looked at Fiss'Q with firelit eyes, twinned pools of petulance and passion, and, before Fiss'Q's eyes, Lyra faded from view. Fiss'Q jumped to her feet to catch her, but her hands passed right through her, her voice a whisper as she vanished.

"Farewell, Senator," Lyra said, and then she disappeared.

Fifteen

Darha had heard the Night's Violin playing. She'd woven a spell to assist her in tracking the thing, drawn from the shadows, themselves. When the notes were played, Darha could sense its location and direction, like the way one could divine the drop of a rock into a body of water by the course of the ripples it made.

In this case, the rock had been dropped at Fiss'Q's townhome, and Darha spirited herself in that direction, only to find that the music and the Violin had vanished.

All the same, she made her way to Fiss'Q's, traveling by rooftop this time, mindful that her spell-weaving had cost her another rune on her hand. Eight lives left.

She saw Fiss'Q cursing, calling out for the Black Bard, and giving orders to her servants. It would have been an opportune moment to strike, but Darha considered something else as she stood on that neighboring rooftop, watching the Shadowlander conduct her business. Perhaps the Violin was out of reach for now, but it didn't mean that Darha did not have anything to trade. She steeled herself and spoke up.

"Shadowlander," Darha said, and Fiss'Q stopped, recognizing her voice. In that moment, Darha felt the familiar thrill of confronting danger, for there were few things more terrifying than a Shadowlander turning their other-worldly eyes onto a person with harmful intentions.

"Shadowmancer," Fiss'Q said. "Come to finish what you'd started?"

"No," Darha said. "I came to talk."

Fiss'Q parted the Veil and fetched her sword. Darha could see this with her own Shadowsight, and smiled to herself, for the Shadowlander feared her, and there was solace in that fear. It was nice to be feared, rather than disregarded.

She saw Fiss'Q fly up at her and part the Veil again, and the two of them stood on the rooftop, regarding one another by the moonlight—the Shadowlander with her black greatsword, ever the lean and lethal silhouette. And the Shadowmancer, wearing a night-black cloak, her silver eyes glittering.

"What do you want to talk about?" Fiss'Q asked.

"I've come to make peace," Darha said. "And to offer something in trade, as a sign of good faith."

Fiss'Q smiled at her and to herself, her fangs dimpling her lip.

"Go on," Fiss'Q said.

"My contract with the Obsidianders died with Barvikh in the harbor," Darha said. "Or, let me just say that I'm not the sort to carry it through to bitter end for the sake of another. Barvikh's father called me a witch, and would betray me the moment he'd gotten what he wanted."

"What *was* your contract, precisely?" Fiss'Q asked, glancing around them. She suspected a trap, and Darha didn't blame her.

"To recover the Night's Violin," Darha said. "And to destroy Arokhnai."

"Quite a contract," Fiss'Q said, gripping her sword tighter.

"At the time, it seemed the right move," Darha said.

"And now?"

"I've had a change of heart," Darha said. "Having walked and stalked the streets of Arokhnai, I wish to petition for asylum."

Fiss'Q had not expected this, from the look in her ruby eyes. Darha could see her mind working, plotting, scheming, weighing, evaluating.

"Asylum?" Fiss'Q asked. "Why?"

"You already divined that I'm from Ansible," Darha said. "I grew up there. And when you're from Ansible, you hear things about Arokhnai. Everyone hears stories about Arokhnai. That you Shadowlanders cavort in the darkness with your dark Prince, consorting with demons. You are assassins and manipulators."

"I've heard them all before," Fiss'Q said. "So let me guess—now that you've spent some time here, you see that those stories were just that—stories."

Darha nodded.

"When I fled Ansible, I threw my lot in with Uriokh out of necessity and desperation," Darha said.

"From the proverbial frying pan to the fire," Fiss'Q said.

"No doubt," Darha said. "But I did what I had to do to survive. Something you've probably never had to do in your blessedly immortal life."

Fiss'Q smiled a sorrowful smile. She had no idea the sacrifices Fiss'Q had made to be who and what she was.

"An immortal life must begin somewhere, Darha," Fiss'Q said. "The question is whether it begins from the moment of immortality, or whether it starts the moment you do."

Darha had no interest in the metaphysical machinations of the Shadowlander. She merely wanted sanctuary in Arokhnai. She held up her hands, showing her radiant fingernails, rune-bedecked as they were, with two nails dark.

"My life is measured out for me," Darha said. "I know what I have left, from what I've stolen from your Shadow Prince. A blessing? A curse?"

Fiss'Q sighed.

"The Prince of Shadows is a god of thieves," Fiss'Q said. "If you didn't already know, there it is. He would find your opportunism…intriguing."

"Either way," Darha said. "I don't want to run out my life as the errand girl for the ambitions of greedy men. I want to live."

"As do we all," Fiss'Q said. "What do you propose?"

"Sanctuary," Darha said. "In return, I will help you against your enemies, provided you treat on my behalf with your master, so I do not die."

Fiss'Q privately thought the Prince of Shadows would love Darha Lonai.

"So He does not kill you," Fiss'Q said. "Again, killing you would be the last thing He would consider, trust me."

"I wish I could," Darha said. "I took up Shadowmancy because it was a place no one else would go. I did it to make my own way in Ansible. It's all I know, but it's not all that I am. I can help you. Your people. Your city."

"Why the change of heart, truly?" Fiss'Q asked. "What stratagem is this?"

"My heart is unchanged," Darha said. "But I'm no fool. I could have killed you when we last crossed, Senator. You know that. I didn't. I had told you then that I wanted to talk, but you were otherwise preoccupied."

"It wasn't a good time for a chat," Fiss'Q said. Despite Lyra's healing, the memory of the wounds would linger for Fiss'Q. Fiss'Q did not know what to think. The Shadow Senate would consider the Shadowmancer a threat. Unique among magi, she could truly hurt Shadowlanders. The young woman was a living weapon. The Senate had dealt with Shadowmancers in the past, when they threatened Arokhnai's interests. The easiest, perhaps most sensible thing to do was to kill her right there. And yet, Fiss'Q stayed her hand.

"If I had your pledge to do no harm to the people of Arokhnai, it would go a long way," Fiss'Q said. "If your word is good, and this is not some elaborate ruse you've arranged."

"My word is good," Darha said. "I'm a selfish opportunist, Senator. I'm seeking this opportunity for myself, and am prepared to pay dearly for it. I didn't have to come to you this way. I could have simply attacked you while you mourned the loss of your lady love."

Fiss'Q's gaze hardened at being so transparent to the Shadowmancer. How used the Shadowlanders were to seeing into others' hearts and souls. To have another able to gaze into theirs was both unfamiliar and unwelcome. It made Darha smile, that bit of leverage she possessed.

"I haven't lost her," Fiss'Q said. "She's lost to me."

"But not to me," Darha said. "I can find her. Whenever she plays, I can find her. But not without cost."

Darha flexed her glittery fingernails.

"So, that's your deal? You help me find Lyra, and I let you shelter in Arokhnai?"

"No," Darha said. "The deal is threefold: first, you let me reside safely in Arokhnai; second, you protect my life from the wrath of your Shadow Prince; third, I agree not to harm anyone in Arokhnai. But that's not all I bring to the table."

Fiss'Q cocked her eyebrow.

"There's more?" Fiss'Q asked. "You are generous, Shadowmancer."

"This last bit, I would not sell cheaply," Darha said. "I want to become a Shadowlander."

"I'm surprised it took you so long to ask," Fiss'Q said. "But you must know that it's far more dangerous than anything you could imagine."

Darha smiled back at her, a predatory thing.

"I have a vivid imagination," Darha said.

"The Prince of Shadows is capricious," Fiss'Q said. "He does not simply take all who come to Him."

"Nonetheless, it is my price," Darha said. "For the information I have is of vital importance to the survival of Arokhnai."

"All I can promise is an audience," Fiss'Q said. "The Prince may not take you. Or, He may love you and steal you away from this world. He's done it before."

Fiss'Q could not imagine anyone more dangerous than a

Shadowmancer turned Shadowlander. She would be even deadlier than she already was. That is, if the Prince even accepted her. He may have been so taken with her that He might take her as His consort. Wouldn't that be a thing?

"I'm willing to accept that," Darha said. "And I would abide by my word not to harm anyone from Arokhnai."

"What are you offering in trade?" Fiss'Q asked.

"First, I want your word that you'll give me that audience," Darha said.

Fiss'Q knew that it was something she'd have to take up with her mentor, Q'rr'k, who was Shadow Lord of Arokhnai. If he didn't already know about Darha, the prospect would alternately entice and repel.

"I can give you audience with Lord Q'rr'k, my mentor, and our current Shadow Lord," Fiss'Q said. "It would be up to him to decide if you rated an audience with the Prince of Shadows."

Darha hadn't expected to be even given that much. She assumed Fiss'Q would jealously guard the secret of her power, the way a wizard of Ansible would protect their arcane knowledge.

"Very well," Darha said. "An audience with Lord Q'rr'k."

"I'll make the arrangements," Fiss'Q said. "Now, what do you offer in trade?"

Darha took a breath. It was almost her last card to play, but she hoped that it would be a decisive one in these negotiations.

"The Obsidianders have a sent a war fleet to Arokhnai," Darha said. "They will be here in three days. Under the command of Lord Abbasa, himself."

Darha could see that the Shadowlander had not expected that.

"Three days?" Fiss'Q asked. "Your confederates?"

"Of course," Darha said. "It was part of my arrangement with Lord Abbasa. I would recover the Night's Violin and use it to destroy Arokhnai's defenses. He would send his fleet and seize the city. But, as the Violin has escaped my grasp, and, to be honest, having seen it in action and its effect on me, it forces me to consider another path."

"Treacherous," Fiss'Q said.

"One cannot treat honorably with Slavelords, Senator," Darha said. "But in your free republic, I see something more hopeful and promising than in the other cities. I would not like that to be snuffed out by the likes of Lord Abbasa. I have one other condition, however, which I hope would be a sign of my good faith."

The Shadowlander nodded after a moment.

"Go on," Fiss'Q said.

"Do not simply sink the ships," Darha said. "Rather, free the slaves aboard the vessels. They are war galleys, packed with galley slaves."

"You don't seem the type to care, Darha," Fiss'Q said.

"No one should be a slave," Darha said. "I know that firsthand. Unlike you, I grew up in Slaver Cities, not in free and happy Arokhnai."

"How can I be sure this is not some trap?" Fiss'Q asked.

"I suppose you can't," Darha said. "Screened as I am from your Shadowsight, you cannot know my motivations. You'll just have to trust me."

Darha smirked at Fiss'Q, her silver eyes glinting in the darkness.

"Your motivations are highly suspect," Fiss'Q said.

"What I want more than anything is a home of my own," Darha said. "A place of peace where I can do my research in safety. Arokhnai *is* that place. Having seen her, would

I really want to see her enslaved by the preening, fuming Obsidianders? What's more, a defeat of their war fleet would tip the balance of power in the region, yes? I know that Arokhnai has to deal with their ships as you trade."

"Yes," Fiss'Q said. "It would. The loss of Lord Abbasa would set them back immeasurably."

"I'm prepared to offer a final boon," Darha said. "If your Shadow Lord meets with me and finds me suitable for the needs of your Prince, I'll make war on the Obsianders, as only I am able."

"What about that life of peace and safety you wanted only moments ago?" Fiss'Q asked.

"The destruction of the Slavelords of Uriokh would bring lasting peace to the region," Darha said. "You know I'm right about that. I have an interest in seeing their destruction, for my own well-being."

Fiss'Q, of course, knew that she was. Proximity alone made the Obsidian Island a threat to Arokhnai. And their warships plied the same waters, their slave-taking was a rapacious enterprise. The Shadowmancer's silver-eyed gaze saw right through her, and she smiled.

"Think of it, Senator," Darha said. "Another Slaver City to be liberated. Beautiful Arokhnai wouldn't stand so alone as she had before. In the time of the Manticore, that sort of alliance would be a most welcome thing. You'd control all sea trade in and out of the Sorian Sea."

"We would," Fiss'Q said. "Alright, Darha. You've given me a lot to think about. I must make arrangements. You can stay at my home, so long as you swear to abide by your word not to harm anyone in Arokhnai, starting with my servants."

Darha couldn't believe she'd made it this far with the formidable Fiss'Q.

"I swear it," Darha said. "No harm to you or anyone in Arokhnai. And all that we discussed will come to pass."

Fiss'Q rested her greatsword on her shoulder and held out a hand. Darha shook it, and the deal was struck by the cold light of the moon.

Sixteen

The Obsidiander war fleet was nearing Arokhnai when the Shadowmancer appeared on the deck of the *Aggressor*, Lord Abbasa's flagship. Abbasa stood at the bow of his boat, watching for any sign of other vessels. He'd been hoping to see sign of his son's boat for days, now. They were overdue.

"Well, you finally returned," Abbasa said, glaring at the sorceress, who stood at the bow with Abbasa. "Where is my son?"

"He's dead," Darha said. "Sent to the bottom of the harbor by the Black Bard, in fact, along with the rest of his crew. She burned them alive."

"You came here to tell me this?" Abbasa asked, glaring hard at Darha.

"I did," Darha said. "And to say goodbye."

"Goodbye?" Abbasa said, reaching for his sword.

Darha stepped back. Darha could see the legion of Shadowlanders approaching the ships, and she smiled. It would be a good thing to see, more so with Shadowsight. There were hundreds of them, moving like luminous darts, bearing their own weapons, luminous to one with the Shadowsight, but invisible to the hapless Obsidianders, who had no idea what was coming. This shadow army moved with speed and silence toward the war fleet, in a great wedge formation that arced as it neared the war galleys, a Shadowlander landing on each boat unseen, from the safety of the Veil.

It was a stirring sight, and Darha felt privileged to have witnessed it. Never had so many Shadowlanders sallied forth this way, the *Vladinakhti,* the Shadow Warriors, themselves, which described their way of fighting as well.

The Veil parted, and Fiss'Q appeared, bearing her greatsword, which she sank into the chest of Lord Abbasa before he could even draw his own. The Slavelord gasped, coughing up blood, and she yanked the blade free of him before the stunned gaze of his men.

There was similar commotion aboard the other Obsidiander vessels, and Darha knew that the other Shadow Warriors were attacking those as well. All around her, the here and now was dotted with the shades of Obsidianders, stunned at their sudden, irredeemable fate.

Fiss'Q vanished into the shadows and began the bobbing *Vladinakhti* style of attack for which the Shadowlandish were known, her sword lancing out from the shadows to spear and hew at the panicking Obsidianders, only to disappear a moment later, back into the shadows.

Darha knelt by the dying Lord Abbasa, prying the gold rings from his fingers.

"Your reign is ended, Lord Abbasa," Darha said, trying the ring on for size on her thumb. "There will be no invasion of Arokhnai, and you will be thrown into the sea with the rest of your men."

The clatter of swords and spears matched the cries of men, as Fiss'Q concluded her lethal business with them.

The galley slaves looked on in terrified amazement at their position along the length of the warship, oars in hand. Each ship was, to Darha's silver gaze, a torrent of activity as the Shadow Warriors danced between the Veil and the here and now to slay the Obsidianders where they stood. The commotion was absolute, as was the seeming chaos of it, but Darha could discern the order of it all, the fluid, flowing nature of it. It gave her chills to bear such witness.

Fiss'Q finished up Abbasa's warriors in a few more minutes, before reappearing on the bow, bearing her black blade, which was now red with blood. She looked at Darha, who stared back at her. For a moment, Darha feared that the Shadowlander might run her through with her sword, but the Senator just flicked the blood off her sword with a snap of her wrist, and began to speak, addressing the galley slaves on the *Aggressor* with a practiced and pleasantly powerful speaking voice.

"Enslaved people of Uriokh," Fiss'Q said. "I am Senator Fiss'Q. You have been liberated by the Republic of Arokhnai."

The slaves said nothing, before mustering the courage to cheer at the stunning reversal of fortune for them. To have begun the day as slaves and ended it as free men was not what they had expected. Darha could see the joy and excitement flowing off them, as readily as she saw the bewildered shades of the fallen Obsidianders floating away from the battleground. The contrast between life and death, victory and defeat, could not have been more bracing.

The other Obsidiander ships were commandeered as readily by the assembled Shadow Warriors, and the bodies of Uriokh's slavers were thrown into the sea, to feed the sharks, which had been trailing them anyway, as was common with slave ships and war galleys.

Fiss'Q directed the removal of the chains of the galley slaves, and commanded them to row the fleet to Arokhnai on their own power.

Darha looked on, satisfied at what she had wrought. The Night of Long Shadows, as it became known, became a song popularized in Arokhnai when the freed slaves told the story of what they had seen. In Uriokh, word would eventually go out about the loss of Lord Abbasa and the war fleet, and the city descended into a power struggle among the other, lesser slavelords.

The freed slaves of Uriokh numbered nearly 20,000, which was far more than Arokhnai could handle under the circumstances. Rather, the freed galley slaves were paraded through the Emerald District, where they were assembled into the open markets, not as property, but as freemen.

Along the way to the Grand Market, they were given bread and meat and water, where they were sorted out according to where they had come from, and what skills they had in life.

"This is a heroic thing you've done, Shadowmancer," Fiss'Q said, watching the sorting take place from her rooftop deck, with Darha nearby. "Although it poses some challenges for us."

Darha glanced at Fiss'Q.

"I have no doubt Arokhnai can handle any challenges she faces," Darha said.

"We are sorting by profession and by place of origin," Fiss'Q said. "Soldiers, sailors, farmers, merchants, and ar-

tisans, we are offering citizenship and work when they are healthy. There is always a need."

"And the rest?" Darha asked.

"The Northlanders are going to trek home," Fiss'Q said. "We'll send a convoy of vessels north as an escort for them, which is far safer than an overland journey. We are confiscating the best of the Obsidiander warships and are renaming and repainting them as vessels of Arokhnai. We don't use galleys, but they can be useful for us all the same, to guard our coasts."

"You should invade Uriokh now," Darha said. "While their war fleet is taken, while they are in a power struggle over who rules. Now is the time."

"The Shadow Senate will debate these things," Fiss'Q said. "We hardly want to get enmeshed in a war."

"But the war came to you all the same," Darha said.

"What about Lyra?" Fiss'Q asked. "Where is she?"

"She's still in the city," Darha said.

"Here?" Fiss'Q asked, her red eyes flashing.

"For now, yes," Darha said. "She's in the Dreamgardens."

"Thank you," Fiss'Q said, excusing herself. Fiss'Q didn't wait a moment, but parted the Veil, and flew at once to the Dreamgardens.

"Farewell, Senator," Darha said. She felt certain she and Fiss'Q would cross paths again, although she hoped they would do so as allies, and not enemies, if not yet as friends. As she flexed her fingers and looked out across busy Arokhnai, Darha was confident that a better, brighter future awaited her, one of her own design.

✤ ✤ ✤

Seventeen

The Dreamgardens were a particularly beautiful part of Arokhnai, covering a whole city block. In it was a collection of every sort of tree and flower that would grow in the Southlands. The Dreamgardens had been built centuries earlier by Quanch Votilla, a Shadowlander merchant prince, in celebration of a successful trade route he'd established with faraway Stormfist. It was a tradition in Arokhnai to adorn the city with things of beauty to herald its successes. Among citizens of Arokhnai, few had ever exceeded Votilla's accomplishment.

Fiss'Q could see Lyra there in the heart of it, surrounded by hearthwood trees, and fragrant stands of matron's kisses, lover's lament, blueflower, and countless others. She was playing the Night's Violin for some rapt onlookers, performing "The Night of Long Shadows" for them. She had not written the tune, but played it beautifully, all the same.

Fiss'Q watched her play from beyond the Veil, seeing the emotion flow from her, and from the onlookers, and the power of the instrument flaring almost blindingly in the dimness of the Shadowlands. The throb of the magic of the Violin struck a chord in Fiss'Q.

How lovely it was, and how fleeting, as Lyra stopped playing, and warmly received the applause of the city folk. And the coins, as well.

"I thank you," Lyra said, in her grandiose manner. "For the gift of your attention. I'm humbled and honored to be able to play in the Dreamgarden, a place I've only heard about, never seen."

"Play another tune," one of the city folk said, joined by others.

"No," Lyra said. "The day belongs to you, people of Arokhnai, for your great triumph against the slavers of Uriokh. I only wanted to honor that victory in my own small way. And to spend some time at peace in these lovely gardens."

Fiss'Q knew better than to simply appear before the crowd. It would have ruined the mood, and Fiss'Q was never one to do that.

Instead, she watched from the shadows as Lyra put away her instrument, saw the crowd reluctantly disperse, and then chose her proper moment to appear, when Lyra was drinking in the scent of redflower and dreaming of her next journey. She planned to travel far away from here, to the shores of Imperia, and their great capital of Baselika.

She parted the Veil and appeared before Lyra, startling her.

"Fiss'Q," Lyra said, smiling awkwardly yet charmingly. "I knew you'd find me. In fact, I'd lingered in the city when I heard about what happened. To bear witness."

"Of course," Fiss'Q said.

"You have won the day," Lyra said. "From what I hear, a great victory."

"We did," Fiss'Q said. "I would have enjoyed the victory more had you been there beside me. You could have seen

it firsthand, instead of playing another's song to commemorate it."

Lyra smiled a wounded smile, rolling her eyes.

"It's a good tune," Lyra said. "Had I helped you, I would have likely burnt the slave ships to the waterline like I did that one in the harbor, and sent the slaves to their deaths at the bottom of the sea. It would not have occurred to me to have freed them. I would have been caught up in my tune, in my performance, and by the time I'd have realized my mistake, it would have been too late. Another song, entirely."

"Perhaps," Fiss'Q said. "Or maybe you would have changed your tune and performed a greater miracle, still, something to dwarf what you did at Valdikan."

"I'm still not a hero, Senator," Lyra said. "It's not in my blood. And you've got a war on your hands."

"We could use you," Fiss'Q said. "And I need you."

Lyra reached out and caressed Fiss'Q's cheek with her musician's fingers. Delicate but strong in their artful way. The feel of them brought Fiss'Q both pleasure and pain.

"I believe you really do," Lyra said. "But it's too steep a price for me to remain here. I'm no slave to duty, Senator. I'm a free woman, and I must go where I wish. You must respect that."

Fiss'Q's heart was wounded at Lyra's cavalier nature.

"Is there nothing I can do or say to make you stay?" Fiss'Q asked. She was not used to being in such a position, to having to beg.

"You are the hero of Arokhnai," Lyra said. "Not me."

"I'm not asking you to be a hero this time," Fiss'Q said.

"But you were," Lyra said. "What's more, if I were to stay with you, I would have to be. I was not made to stand in your shadow, Fiss'Q."

Tears filled Fiss'Q's eyes. She could not remember the last time she'd cried, and thinking of that made her cry all the more.

"The Manticore will kill you," Fiss'Q said. "I could protect you. I *will* protect you."

"You cannot," Lyra said. "Your first love is Arokhnai and her people. And I know that. I don't blame you. It's exquisite. All of it is."

In the Dreamgardens, the rest of Arokhnai was a world away. It was only Fiss'Q and Lyra, and Fiss'Q's pain, in the cool shadow of a massive hearthwood tree, its great leaves shading them from the merciless Southland sun.

Wounded, Fiss'Q felt pain rise up in her heart. She could simply take the Violin from Lyra. As a Senator of Arokhnai, she was empowered to do what she needed to in order to protect the city. She could do this and send Lyra out of the city as an exile. What's more, she should.

"I love you, Lyra," Fiss'Q said. "I know it's foolish, but I do."

"And I love you," Lyra said, embracing her. "I'll write a song about you, about us. Something to remember you by when I'm far away, in Imperia, or Stormfist, or even Mandria."

"Please," Fiss'Q said. "Please stay away from Mandria, Lyra. You torment me by even saying that."

The Mandrians would burn Lyra at the stake and the Dragon would consume the Night's Violin, making its power His own. Even the idea of it filled her with dread.

"I'm born to bear witness to the world," Lyra said. "That is my fate. I watch, and I make songs of what I see. I could

stay here by your side, and it would be a beautiful life. We'd make a lovely duet, you and me. But I know myself, and some part of me would resent being tethered here. I need to see the world, whatever that brings."

As tears journeyed down her shadowed face, Fiss'Q shook her head.

"It will be small comfort when the Manticore's spitting you over a hearthfire," Fiss'Q said. "The life you could have led."

"It's mine to live and die for," Lyra said, leaning in to give Fiss'Q a lingering kiss in the hulking shadow of the hearthwood tree.

Lyra parted from Fiss'Q, her grey eyes searching Fiss'Q's forlorn face, and she backed away, reaching for the Violin.

Fiss'Q's tear-stained face hardened with her heart.

"I cannot let you run off with it," Fiss'Q said, and she lunged for the Night's Violin, snatching it up before Lyra could react, who cried out and threw herself at the Shadowlander.

Fiss'Q parted the Veil, the stolen instrument in her grasp, with rage boiling up in the Black Bard in coruscating waves. Fiss'Q had not wanted to do this, but it would have been a terrible mistake for her to let her leave with the instrument. As painful as it was, heroism demanded such sacrifices.

"Fiss'Q!" Lyra screamed, her voice carrying that strange tone mundane voices always did in the Shadowlands.

Wasting no time, Fiss'Q flew from Lyra, and to Q'rr'k. She went to his city villa, which seamlessly blended light and shadow in the most agreeable of ways. He was waiting for her in his atrium garden, near a fountain where the

Shadow Prince cavorted, leering at them while brandishing a cup from which flowed the fountain's water.

Q'rr'k saw her coming, and Fiss'Q parted the Veil, standing before him. He looked as elegant as ever, wearing a purple silk robe embroidered with gold dragons that wound around the pattern in serpentine circles. His handsome face regarded her with a dram of compassion.

"You recovered it?" Q'rr'k asked.

"I did," she replied. "That was difficult. Painful."

"Of course," Q'rr'k said. "But you had to do it. Let me see it."

Fiss'Q opened the case, and the beautiful instrument was visible within, on the blue velvet that bedded it. Q'rr'k took it out and turned it over in his hands. Neither of them were musicians, neither able to play the thing, and neither of them was foolish enough to try.

"What of the Black Bard?" Q'rr'k asked.

"In the Dreamgardens," Fiss'Q said. "Cursing me. Hating me."

"Maybe she'll write a song about you," Q'rr'k said. "This was the right thing to do, my darling."

"We shall see," Fiss'Q said. "The Manticore is still going to hunt for her."

"Yes," Q'rr'k said. "But with this, *we* might be able to end *him*."

"I hope so," Fiss'Q said. Her heart ached in more ways than she could say. She would have rather done anything than what she'd done.

"I can't believe Farro even parted with it," Q'rr'k said.

"It's a burden as much as it is a boon," Fiss'Q said. "Part of its curse, I imagine."

"Still, I *never* would have parted with it," Q'rr'k said.

"That's because you're you," Fiss'Q said.

"Besides," Q'rr'k said, putting it back in its case, closing the clasps. "You're going to hold onto it for me."

Fiss'Q thought he was joking, but his violet eyes and earnest expression showed that he was not.

"Me? I can't possibly," Fiss'Q said.

"And yet, you must," Q'rr'k replied. "I trust you, Fiss'Q. More than I trust myself. That you even followed through on this shows me just how trustworthy you are. I want you to reach out to the Sylvanni. Tell them we have it, and that we'll give it back to them, for safekeeping."

"Truly?" Fiss'Q asked.

"Yes," Q'rr'k said. "It's theirs. They made the thing. I'd like to think if we did so, we'd earn some favors with them, ones we may need to trade in later."

Q'rr'k was always thinking of the gameboard of statesmanship, and she loved him for it.

"A good plan," Fiss'Q said.

"Once this business with Uriokh is ended, I'll want you to lead a delegation to Sylvannia," Q'rr'k said. "To arrange the return of the Violin. You're the only one I trust with this."

"I'm honored, Q'rr'k," Fiss'Q said.

Fiss'Q took back the Violin, feeling the weight of it, like an anchor, around her very soul. The last thing she wanted was the instrument. But maybe that's why Q'rr'k had decided that. Her mind was already working on the prospect of a trek to Sylvannia. There could be no arena more challenging than that, and that challenge excited her.

"Besides, I have enough to worry about with that Shadowmancer you treated with," Q'rr'k said. "The last thing I want is the distraction of that *thing* in my villa."

Fiss'Q could not be sure whether he was referring to the Violin or the Shadowmancer, and didn't press him.

"She helped us save the city," Fiss'Q said. "And she seems sincere in her motivations. She means to make war on Uriokh."

"Yes," Q'rr'k said. "Can hardly blame her for that."

"You can't possibly make her one of us," Fiss'Q said. Q'rr'k smiled at her, his becoming smile she well-remembered from their past together, when they shared a bed and endless evenings.

"We shall see," Q'rr'k said. "The Prince of Shadows may take a liking to her. You did well for Arokhnai in these matters, Fiss'Q. He has noticed, and approves. Besides, she's contrived to have that luthier, Kaden, make a replica of the Night's Violin—a counterfeit, to throw the Manticore off the scent, as it were. It's going to make an appearance in Uriokh, when it's ready. If I understood her, she also intends to use it as a ruse to pit the remaining slavelords against one another—a worthless prize for them to fight each other for. All while you are secreting it back to Sylvannia."

Fiss'Q managed a smile at that. Darha had the instinct for intrigue inherent in the Shadowmancer. She'd fit well in Arokhnai. She'd be in Q'rr'k's bed in no time at all, if she wasn't already.

"You should feel good about the day, Fiss'Q," Q'rr'k said. "This is a triumph for us. I've wanted us to have some leverage with the Sylvanni for centuries. This will give us that. A delegation with them would be monumental."

Fiss'Q felt anything but good, but the favor of the Shadow Prince was hard-won, and if Q'rr'k said it, she was confident there was at least some truth to it, somewhere to be found. The Shadow Lord reached out and patted her on the shoulder gently.

"To live in the shadow is to carry a multitude of burdens, my darling," Q'rr'k said. "This is only one of very many you'll carry with you before you one day become Shadow Lord of Arokhnai."

Fiss'Q could not imagine replacing Q'rr'k, who simply smiled at her.

"Not for a very long time," Q'rr'k said. "At least that's my hope."

"And mine," Fiss'Q said, embracing her former mentor, lover, and tutor. He hugged her back. Their bond would never fray. She counted on that.

"Go home, get rest," Q'rr'k said. "Bathe in the freshly-forged shadows of your broken heart, and we'll talk again later."

"I'll do my best," Fiss'Q said, parting the Veil and slipping away.

"You always do," Q'rr'k said, watching her go.

Eighteen

Lyra was waiting for her in front of her townhome. An'Alta would not let her in, and the Black Bard was crying out in front of her townhome, for any who would listen. Her oratory would not be denied.

"Fiss'Q!" Lyra said, her lovely voice carrying along the street. "I know you're in there. Come out!"

Fiss'Q could see that her anger was rising from her in great waves, and she passed within her home, to her Shadowvault, in a part of her home that only she could access, as it was sealed off from the here and now by strong walls. In that little room, Fiss'Q entered, parting the Veil, abruptly cutting off the complaints of Lyra.

Within that room was a silver strongbox, a blackwood table, and a matching chair. Fiss'Q took a seat and put on a pair of soft, black leather gloves that rested on the table. She then turned to open the strongbox, and placed the Night's Violin within it, atop the other treasures Fiss'Q had placed within it over the years. She closed the strongbox, flipping the latch to secure it.

It would be safe there until she traveled to Sylvannia. Such a journey, she could hardly imagine. She'd never been there before, and wondered how she'd be received.

There were no more formidable schemers than the Sylvanni. Fiss'Q would plan it carefully.

She parted the Veil and again heard the chorus of Lyra's complaints, felt the fire of her wounded rage, and floated out to see her. She owed her that much.

Fiss'Q appeared before her.

"Harpy!" Lyra said. "Monster! Thief! You stole it from me! Give it back!"

"I can't," Fiss'Q said. "I simply cannot."

Lyra's grey eyes were aflame with fury, her face a snarl.

"You betrayed me," Lyra said. "For all of your talk of love, you betrayed me."

"I warned you," Fiss'Q said.

"You warned me," Lyra said. "Duplicitous fiend. I curse the day I set foot in Arokhnai."

"You came to me," Fiss'Q said. "You came to me for help. I've helped you."

"You've damned me," Lyra said. "Where is it? What have you done with it?"

"It's safe," Fiss'Q said. "I'm keeping it safe."

Lyra threw herself at Fiss'Q, drawing her rapier and swinging at her in the Sylvan-touched style she'd learned. Fiss'Q let the steel blade strike her, for ordinary steel could find no purchase on a Shadowlander.

The Black Bard lunged and stabbed at Fiss'Q until she was out of breath, throwing down her sword and crying into her hands. Her tears pained Fiss'Q even more, but she remained resolute in the face of the deluge.

"You said that the Manticore would come for me," Lyra said. "That he'd seek his revenge on me."

"And he will," Fiss'Q said. "The Black Bard of Valdikan will know no peace so long as the Manticore lives."

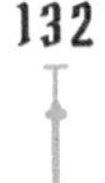

"By taking the Violin from me, you condemn me to death," Lyra said.

"No," Fiss'Q said. "But there's a way out for you, if you want it. Simply retire the Black Bard until the Manticore has been dealt with."

Lyra's rage grew even greater, as incredible as that seemed to Fiss'Q. She was a fountain of fury, spitting mad.

"Never," Lyra said. "My name and reputation is bound up in who I am, and what I did. I can't believe you'd even suggest that. I am the Black Bard. I will always be her."

"Just trying to keep you alive," Fiss'Q said. "Since you're determined to put yourself at risk."

"Oh, no," Lyra said. "You wanted me in Arokhnai, Senator? I'm here. I'm here until the Violin is returned to me. I'm here to sing songs of your theft and betrayal of me. I'll sing out against you. I'll make rousing tunes that impugn what you call your honor. You'll be my malevolent muse."

Fiss'Q picked up Lyra's slender sword and handed it to her, hilt first. Lyra snatched it up and waved it at her again.

"I dedicate this first song to Senator Fiss'Q," Lyra said. "I call it 'Lyra's Lament.'"

Lyra broke into song, her beautiful voice carrying forth from the street, turning heads as she did so.

> *"Alone in the world, and finding her way,*
> *the singer she came to this city one day.*
> *She met up with Fiss'Q,*
> *and they had a tryst,*
> *and the shadows they stole her away.*
> *The Night's Violin was her only sin,*
> *and the shadows they stole her away."*

Fiss'Q smiled sadly at Lyra and parted the Veil, floating up to her townhome, to her rooftop deck, where Lyra's lovely voice carried up like a serenade, the anger and grief boiling up in waves from her song, the melody going on and on, Lyra throwing lyric after lyric after her, each fusillade more damning than the next.

Fiss'Q took to her bed, alone once again, and slept while Lyra sang out her rage and hate on the streets below, for any able to hear her. At least here, in Arokhnai, hating her with every breath, Fiss'Q knew that Lyra would be safe.

FINIS

A Note on the Type

The text of this book is set in Adobe Jenson Pro, an old-style serif typeface drawn for Adobe Systems by its chief type designer Robert Slimbach. Its Roman styles are based on a text face cut by Nicolas Jenson in Venice around 1470, and its italics are based on those created by Ludovico Vicentino degli Arrighi fifty years later.

Nicholas Jenson (1420–1480) was a French engraver, pioneer, printer and type designer who carried out most of his work in Venice, Italy. Jenson acted as Master of the French Royal Mint at Tours, and is credited with being the creator of one of the finest early Roman type faces. Nicholas Jenson has been something of an iconic figure among students of early printing since the nineteenth century when the aesthete William Morris praised the beauty and perfection of his roman font. Jenson is an important figure in the early history of printing and a pivotal force in the emergence of Venice as one of the first great centers of the printing press.

Ludovico Vicentino degli Arrighi (1475–1527) was a papal scribe and type designer in Renaissance Italy. He turned to printing in 1524 and designed his own italic typefaces for his work, which were widely emulated. His last printing was dated shortly before the sack of Rome (1527), during which he was probably killed.

Composed by Clever Crow Consulting and Design,
Pittsburgh, Pennsylvania

Acknowledgments

I would like to thank all of my readers, who offered their time, attention, and opinions to the writing and revision of this book. I would also like to thank Christine Marie Scott of Clever Crow Consulting and Design in Pittsburgh for her wonderful cover art and her invaluable assistance with the layout of these pages.

About the Author

Dane Vale lives in Chicago, where he conjures up Sword & Sorcery and Fantasy fiction when he's not relentlessly critiquing his twin brother's writing. He owns at least one spear, dodges drunk texts from Dionysus, and believes that there should be more megaliths in America. He cooks Italian food with verve, and has a bond with wolves and crows. His favorite cities are Knossos, Carthage, Constantinople, Venice, and Paris. **RealDaneVale.com**

NOSETOUCH PRESS

Nosetouch Press is an independent book publisher tandemly based in Chicago and Pittsburgh. We are dedicated to bringing some of today's most energizing fiction to readers around the world.

Our commitment to classic book design in a digital environment brings an innovative and authentic approach to the traditions of literary excellence.

*We're Out There™

NOSETOUCHPRESS.COM

Science Fiction | Fantasy | Urban Fantasy | Horror
Folk Horror | Occult | Supernatural | Gothic | Weird

Visit realdanevale.com
for interviews, maps, and more
from Sagas of Irth!